Murder In Key West
4

Murder In Key West
4

Murder and Mayhem
In Paradise

Edited by Shirrel Rhoades

ABSOLUTELY AMAZING eBOOKS

ABSOLUTELY AMAZING eBOOKS

Published by Whiz Bang LLC, 926 Truman Avenue, Key West, Florida 33040, USA.

For information contact:
Publisher@AbsolutelyAmazingEbooks.com

ISBN-13: 978-1945772443 (Absolutely Amazing Ebooks)
ISBN-10: 1945772441

Yes, here (count 'em) is the fourth volume of *Murder In Key West*. As usual, its publication coincides with the fourth annual Mystery Fest Key West, a conclave of famous writers, aspiring writers, and mystery fans. This book is again dedicated to them.

Murder In Key West
4

Murder In Key West 4

INTRODUCTION

Key West is the southernmost city in the continental United States. It is an end-of-the-road town. So it should be no surprise that bad guys, spies, insurgents, drug smugglers, and undercover cops wind up on this faraway island. That makes for interesting crimes, occasional murders, and shady goings-on.

That is the inspiration of this anthology series, *Murder In Key West*.

Writers come here too. Either as visitors or sometimes residents. And they write about this rash of murder and mayhem. Or they invent stories that *could* have happened in Key West.

Yes, the island offers palm trees and beaches and sunny weather. But its dark alleys and seedy bars are a breeding ground for dark deeds.

You'll read about them herein.

- Shirrel Rhoades
Key West

Vendetta

R. K. Simpson

More than fifty years ago a stranger came to my grandparents' house in Key West late one afternoon and knocked on the screen door. I was then ten years old and home alone. I went to the door and looked up at the person, but the sun at that moment was directly behind him. I shielded my eyes and tried to look straight at him, but the sun was too bright, and his face was cast in shadow. Now, all these years later, knowing what I do, it seems fitting that the faceless form I saw that afternoon, framed in a screen door, is my most lasting impression of the man who claimed to be my father and whom I never saw again.

He said, "Hey, Son, I'm Maynard Bandy."

"Hello," I said, squinting at him.

"Are you Rupert?"

I nodded.

"I'm your Paw, boy, and you're my son." His voice cracked and he nervously picked up a pebble from the ground and tossed it away. Then, as if to be certain he said, "Your last name's Bandy, ain't it?"

I nodded again.

"Pretty much seals the deal," he said. "You *are* my son." As he spoke, he reached out and tried to pull the screen door open, but it was latched. When he did that I saw him briefly. He looked tired and his overalls were too big for him.

"I can't let you in, Mister. My Mama said so. It's one of the rules when I'm home alone."

"Just wanted to shake hands, Son, but you're doin'

right by Mazie," he said. "You doin' good at school too? Got a good teacher?" We talked about school for a while then fell silent. Finally, Mr. Bandy said, "How'd you like to go get a soda or an ice cream?"

"I can't. That's another rule," I said.

"Well, Son, I figure it's time fer me to be goin' then. Was nice to meet you, really. You're a fine lookin' boy." I watched him through the screen as he walked slowly back to his pickup. He turned and waved at me twice and just before he slid into the truck he shouted, "Take care, ya hear?"

When my Mama came home from work and I told her Maynard Bandy had come to visit me, she just stood there with her jaw hanging down. Since she didn't say anything, I asked her right away if he really was my father and she shouted, "Yes, and don't you ever ask me that again!" That was the first time I had asked her about him and first time she had yelled at me, ever. She didn't eat any supper that evening and went to bed early without saying good night to me or her Mama and Daddy. The next morning she came downstairs cool and collected and explained that she had married Maynard in high school, he was a musician and he had chosen a life on the road instead of a life with us. Lastly, she told me in no uncertain terms she didn't want to talk about him again and we didn't until Mama was dying and I was nearly twenty-five.

I thought about him often though because, despite what Maynard and Mama said, I couldn't shake the feeling that he was not my father. We certainly didn't look alike. Maynard was dark skinned, had black hair and brown eyes, and I was a redhead with blue eyes. Moreover, I had no feeling of kinship for him.

About a year after meeting Maynard, I was awakened late one night by my grandparents, J.T. and

Ella Chambliss. They had left their bedroom door open and were arguing about their daughter Mazie, who got pregnant with me when she was eighteen. J.T. was saying it drove him crazy that Mazie still refused to tell him who the father of her child was. At first I thought I was dreaming because the comment made no sense: we all knew it was Maynard Bandy. Mama and I were carrying his family name, after all. Then J.T. rolled out his theory that Mazie had been raped, which was something I didn't know about at my age, but I sensed it was important because Ella became quite upset.

"Let's just back away from this discussion right now," she said. "If you start on this again I won't be able to sleep."

J.T. took her point, but he apparently needed the last word because he added, "You can bet your last buck, Ella, if I ever find out who he is, I'll kill the sonovabitch." This threat made goose bumps stand up on my neck because J.T. had killed before and I had no doubt he could do it again.

"Well, I'm glad you don't know who he is then," Ella shot back in a shaky voice, "because that's exactly what I'd be afraid of." Then she paused. I waited and listened. Finally, Ella said in a voice no longer shaky, "I love you, J.T., more than you know, but I couldn't live with you if I knew you had murdered someone. I would leave you if you did. Have no doubt." From my perspective, that was the ultimate threat. I didn't want to move away; I didn't want them to divorce; and I was deathly afraid I'd end up in an orphanage.

I lived with this confusion over my identity through my childhood, my adolescence, and into my early adult years. I could see no way to resolve it. Maynard's name was forbidden in our house because he had left Mama and me. It was such a touchy subject I didn't dare ask anyone who knew. And so, I grew up as Maynard Bandy's son while believing I wasn't and wondering who I really was.

Fortunately my granddad, J.T., provided me stability and a role model. I loved him and I knew he loved me, but he was a hard man. He had spent four years as a Marine infantry officer in the Pacific and returned a genuine hero with medals, a crippled leg, and a head full of nightmares. I never heard him talk about those years, but while looking for something in the garage once, I came across the citations that described what he did to earn his medals. Several times when I was alone in the house, I went out to the garage and reread them. I won't go into detail except to say he risked his life over and over again and killed many Japanese soldiers to protect his own men. It's no wonder he still had trouble sleeping. Ella said he had mellowed some since his discharge twelve years ago, but not much. He was one tough guy whose demeanor encouraged obedience and whose standards were high and non-negotiable.

He owned Chambliss Marina, a boat repair facility in the Key West Bight, and had instilled in his workforce the same esprit and dedication he had instilled in his Marines. He was a man of few words and no bullshit, but his employees stayed with him and the business had begun to turn a nice profit. This did not affect J.T.'s appearance or lifestyle though. He stayed fit by working out hard every day. I once saw him take a hundred bucks off a salesman who bet him he couldn't do one hundred push-ups in three minutes. He preferred beer to liquor or wine, staying home to going out, and T-shirts and shorts year round. His only flamboyant attribute was his IQ, which he tried to hide with his questionable grammar and south Florida accent, but the men knew he was smart. He had a Masters in Mechanical Engineering from Georgia Tech and a solution every time they came to him with a problem they could not solve.

Despite all he did for me, the missing generation between us left a gap that reminded me I didn't have a father to sit in a boat with me on a warm afternoon, reeling in a few fish, and discussing things; I couldn't look up to see my father clapping for me at my baseball games. J.T. was a loyal, protective presence in my life, but he didn't engage in long, intimate conversations with me, or probably with anyone. When I touched on topics that were still too personal or close to his time in the Pacific, I felt his warnings and backed off. Probably everyone did.

As I rollercoastered through adolescence, thoughts of my real father faded. When they did come to mind, I just tossed them aside. In college, when I was pretending to be an intellectual, I read some books on the complex relationship between sons and fathers that made me wonder why I wanted to meet him at all. My answers seemed to depend on my mood or the last article I had read, but I knew I was gradually moving toward an acceptance of the fact that he would be a permanent disappointment to me. How could I not be disappointed in a man who never showed the courage or the courtesy to face me and give me some answers?

That was my father issue. Mazie was my mother issue. With her tawny hair and dark brown eyes, her delicate long limbs and neck, she reminded me of a faun, always alert and ready to bolt at the first whiff of danger. Actually, she did bolt once before I was born. She jumped aboard a Greyhound bus and went to Miami without telling anyone. When she finally called to check in, J.T. and Ella pleaded with her to come home, but legally they could not force her to do so. In the end, she stayed quite a long time because someone there was promising to put her in the movies. That didn't happen, of course, and she eventually did come home but she had changed, according to Auntie Bea, my mama's older sister. Mazie had become so anxious and skittish that she had difficulty concentrating and was forgetful. After my birth, Ella and Aunt Bea worried that these traits were not ideal in the mother of a newborn so I became a family care project for the first years of my life, but I was lucky. Auntie Bea loved me without limits from my first day on earth, and as time passed she assumed more and more responsibility for my upbringing.

Bea was born in 1942, just after J.T. left for the Pacific and was four when the war ended and he returned. Although J.T. had seen her only twice during those years, she was much like him, smart, determined and independent. She was a child who never worried her parents. She sailed through high school with excellent grades, then earned both her Bachelor's and Masters' degrees in architecture from the University of Florida. While looking for work after graduation she had a minor bike collision with a high school classmate, Nappy Broward, a handsome, happy lad who had led his high school baseball team to a state championship and who had later joined the Key West Police Department after graduating from Rollins College. Six months later they were married. Bea was thoroughly content with her life until the evening of their fourth anniversary when Nappy was hit and killed by a drunk driver. In true conch fashion, the City gave Bea a job-for-life as its Director of Historical Preservation, but for a long time Bea could summon little interest in life, much less in work. Then, according to Ella, when I was born, Bea's melancholy began to lift. J.T. started calling her Auntie Bea and she began cautiously to reenter the flow of life, not as the carefree girl who had married Nappy, but as a mature, strong woman in need of someone to love. Lucky for me, I was that someone.

Bea loved to tell the story of the first time she saw me. "I went to visit him the day he was born," she would begin, "and I just knew I was here on Earth to love and protect him. I stood behind a glass partition in the hospital and looked at him for seven days, trying to figure how such a small person could touch me so deeply. All's I know was that he did and still does," she would say, flushing slightly.

During my first years, Bea would walk over from her office to give me my noon feedings. I have heard folks say that most days she would return to City Hall with Pablum or green jello in her hair and a spring in her step. Ella said she thought the more time Bea spent with me the happier she was. She began coming over for evening feedings, after which she would gather me in her arms and ease herself into the same chair Ella used to rock Mazie to sleep. She would push off with her toes, back and forth, back and forth, while the creaky floor sang beneath us.

But Bea was not simply a softy who spent her time feeding me and rocking me to sleep. In fact, as a young girl and teenager, she was quite a tomboy. She followed her father around imitating his every move and they often did things together that were not traditional father-daughter activities. Bea told me J.T. started taking her to the pistol range when she was ten years old. He not only taught her how to shoot, but how to break down each of his pistols, oil them, and put them back together. By the time I was going to the range with them, Bea was an even better marksman than J.T. He was proud of her ability on the range, but he admired her even more for her willingness to fight for what she believed in. The first time she felt the sting of sexism, she fought back hard. Her high school principal had written her a note rejecting her request to take a course in shop because she was a girl. She was sixteen and came to Ella in tears. At dinner that night her parents told her, "Don't cry about it, fight him" and she did. She used the principal's own note – and J.T. quietly called a couple of his press pals – to win overwhelming public support for her request, which forced the principal to reconsider. She studied small gasoline engines in shop that year.

By the time I entered school, Bea was my *de facto* mom. Of course Mazie, J.T. and Ella were constants in my life too, but Bea was the one who taught me to read, swim, sail, and shoot a pistol. She did my laundry and introduced me to ice cream. On my eleventh birthday she met me walking home from school. Without explanation, she walked me into her house, asked me to close my eyes, and led me into a room. "Surprise!" she said and I opened my eyes to find she had converted her study into a bedroom for me. It had everything a boy needed: a big closet, a desk and a lamp with an adjustable neck, a picture of the 1980 Florida Gators, my favorite team, and a cabinet with inside lighting to display my glass animal collection. From that moment I had two homes and I stopped worrying about going to an orphanage.

We all worried about Mama though. She had gradually relinquished her maternal responsibilities to Bea, but she wanted to be included in decisions about me and occasionally reminded Bea that I was *her* son. Bea, who was part of the problem and part of the solution, usually handled these situations deftly, as she did the day she gave me my own bedroom. Mama saw this as an attempt to lure me away from my grandparents' house but Bea preempted a serious fuss by suggesting we go to Miami so Mama could look for a used car. This had long been one of her fondest aspirations so she jumped at the chance.

~ ~ ~

Several days later we headed east in darkness. As daybreak approached, the blue-black sky faded to pearl grey, the stars withdrew, and a silver sheen spread across the dark waters of the Atlantic. Moments later, the sun edged above the horizon and threw its beams 30,000 feet into the sky, backlighting the spires of the puffy clouds gathering on the horizon and turning the heavens a lemon-yellow.

Bea told me later that she had been transfixed by what she saw that morning. "I'm not religious," she said in a whisper, "but in the presence of such splendor, I just had to thank God for my many blessings, especially the one in the back seat wearing his Florida Gators baseball hat."

She dropped Mama and me off at the Ford dealership on Flagler Avenue. The Chamblisses had been a Ford family for years because J.T. and the General Manager there were old friends. He bought his pick-up trucks for the Marina there at discounted prices and Bea loved her Mustang convertible. She had called the salesman who sold her the car and arranged for him to take good care of her little sister. "I'll be back in a couple hours," she promised, kissing me on the forehead and waving to her sister.

We turned to face a cement and glass building that looked like a science fiction airport. Mama grabbed my hand and headed directly to the main entrance. She sat me in a metal folding chair and said, "I'm going to go find the salesman who's going to help me. Don't you move a muscle until I come back, hear?"

I sat there for ten minutes watching the green and orange pennants snapping above the lot in the hot Miami wind. Finally, I ran outside to see them up close and as my eyes adjusted to the brightness, they fell upon a low-slung, muscular-looking car that had a chrome search light and chrome strips running from the front fenders to the rear fender skirts. It was silver and to me was as exciting as a rocket ship. I opened the passenger door and climbed in cautiously, sensing that it was off limits to the public. I crawled across the fragrant red leather seat and knelt behind the steering wheel so I could scan all the gauges like an astronaut would. Then I began the countdown to blastoff.

Ten, nine, eight ... I made a *whooshing* blastoff noise, but I shut down the rockets abruptly when the head of a man in a cowboy hat filled the open driver's window. His pale face was so close to mine it startled me. All his blemishes were visible. I saw squiggly blood vessels meandered along the sides of his nose. He had a reddish-brown Vandyke beard and a sickish sweet after-shave scent. When he smiled, which he did during that first eternal moment, it looked painful, like a grimace. But, when I think of him now the first thing that comes to mind are his cold blue eyes. They were hypnotic. When they locked onto my eyes, I could not look away. They were wide set and heavy lidded and their gaze felt invasive.

Despite the proximity of our faces neither he nor I withdrew. We remained motionless and communed silently for a few moments. I was oblivious to the sounds and bustle I had noticed earlier. When he reached through the window and patted my thigh, I wasn't frightened or offended.

Then he moved his hand to my crotch. I froze. As I recall, I simply could not move while he fondled me. I don't know how long it lasted but as he withdrew his hand he spoke his first words to me. "I'm Earl Shifflet, Rupert. Wasn't that fun?"

I felt sick. I was so shaken I couldn't speak, but Mr. Shifflet was not waiting for an answer. He was taking in every feature and expression on my face, every measure of my body. I could feel his eyes crawling all over me like lice and I could see his hand draped directly in front of my chest. I was terrified he was going to lower it to my crotch again. I remember his beautiful white leather coat stitched with swirling dark blue designs and a big chunk of turquoise holding his skinny string tie in place. I concentrated on that stone so I wouldn't cry.

I stole a glance at Mr. Shifflet, hoping to see some sign that he was about to leave, but he startled me again. He'd removed his hat to wipe the sweat from his brow and he looked entirely different because he was bald, except for the light red stubble that marched across the back of his head and merged into his sparse sideburns.

I started to shake. Mr. Shifflet must have sensed that I was near the end of my rope. He tussled my hair as he backed away from the car. Then he came toward me again, leaned close and whispered, "You're dead, kid, if you breathe a word of this to anybody, and I'll know if you do." Then he drew his finger across his throat, turned and walked quickly across the lot and into the building. When he was gone, I leaned out of the window and vomited onto the pavement where he had stood.

I do not remember joining up with Mama and Aunt Bea or much about our trip home. I do remember that on the way I saw three men who looked like Mr. Shifflet. At each sighting, I slammed myself down across the back seat and felt prickles run from my head to my neck. I also remember the ocean shining like molten silver, a harsh, grey sky, heat haze boiling off the highway, and sawgrass shaking fitfully in the hot wind and I recall thinking, "This is like Hell."

I don't know what lasting effects Mr. Shifflet's perversion had on me. I told no one about it, but by then I was good at keeping secrets. My health was good and I did well in school, but Shifflet interrupted my sleep occasionally and always in the same way. I would see him in a dream, close-up format only. He appeared to be talking but there was no sound coming from his lips. My vision of him was always in black and white, but as it faded to its conclusion, his Vandyke beard turned bright red and his eyes took on an icy blue color. This weird transformation never failed to wake me and I awoke angry so I was usually unable to go back to sleep right away.

Over time, I learned about Earl Shifflet by researching him in libraries and public records, but I had to dig; he was not a publicity seeker. I determined that he owned a Ford dealership, a beer distributorship, a good deal of real estate, and a movie studio. In attempting to see into Shifflet's murky world, it was often difficult to draw a distinction between fact and fiction. Some papers described him as the kingpin of south Florida vice and linked him to a murder-for-hire-syndicate; others were more circumspect, possibly due to fear or lack of evidence. Despite numerous run-ins with the law, he had never been charged with a crime. His lawyers certainly knew where the skeletons lay and how to use them.

~ ~ ~

Life rolled on. I studied hard and followed in my granddad's footsteps to Georgia Tech. J.T. had built his business into the biggest boat repair facility in the Keys and told me he would rather give the business to me than sell it. So, after completing my Masters in Mechanical Engineering, I started working fulltime as J.T.'s understudy. Ella, who had dabbled in writing children's stories while teaching second grade, had a book published that did well on the national bestseller lists. Bea became influential statewide in historical preservation matters and we heard that Maynard Bandy had gone to Nashville to seek his fortune. My Mama drifted away mentally and died in her early forties.

She was bedridden her last months and became so thin that as she lay sunk in her mattress you could hardly see her little body beneath the sheet and blanket. She was lucid, though, part of the time. One morning when I was coaxing her to eat, she apologized for being an inadequate mother.

"Mama," I said, "I love you. I don't think of you as inadequate at all." She was making amends and tying up loose ends and it wasn't difficult for me to be charitable. "May I ask you a question now?" I asked, thinking charity might beget honesty.

"Of course you may, Sweetie."

"Was Maynard Bandy really my father?"

She answered so quickly it was as if she had anticipated the question. "No," she said, looking away, "he wasn't. I'm sorry, Rupe, for that too. I bet it's a sin to lie about such an important thing." She seemed to contemplate her own statement before saying, "I'm sorry I did it, but I'd do it again even knowing how difficult it has been to live with the decision."

"But why did you do it? I asked.

"Because it was best for you, Rupie. That was my reason for doing everything I did."

"Best for me? You mean going through life believing some innocent guitar player who came to see me only once was my father? Do you mean that's better than knowing who my father really is?" I asked cynically.

"Much, much better," she said.

"You're not going to tell me who he is, are you?" She shook her head back and forth repeatedly. I didn't have the heart to press her further. "That's okay,

Mama," I said. I wish I had given her a kiss then, but years of distance interfered.

A week later, J.T. and Ella entered my room at Bea's at 6 a.m. and sat down on my bed. I knew why they were there. Ella put her hand on my shoulder and said, "Rupe, your Mama left us last night. I'm sorry."

J.T. bent down and kissed me on the forehead. He had never kissed me before. "Sorry, Lad," he whispered.

~ ~ ~

After Mama's funeral, we all settled into our routines again. The next Sunday morning my grandparents and I were drinking coffee and reading the Sunday papers around their kitchen table. That handsome piece of furniture had borne witness to all the important family discussions in my lifetime and was about to do so again. After my talk with Mama, I had decided to try to confirm what she had told me about Maynard. It was too important to accept at face value.

"We gotta talk, Granddad," I said without preamble.

"What can I do for you, Rupe?" J.T. said.

"I'd like to know who my father is." I could have slipped into the conversation more gracefully, but J.T. was a man of few words and he had taught me well.

It seemed like an hour passed before he said, "So would I, Son, but you should leave that alone. No good'll come of it."

"I'm the one to decide that," I said, again sounding sharper than I intended. "I'm twenty-five and I'll be independent and working for a living soon. If my father is alive, it's for me to decide what to do about him."

"You sound like your Mama talking, Son." Then he looked me straight in the eye and said, "Ella and I don't know who your father is ... or was. What's more, we believe your father could damn well have contacted you by now if he was interested in you and we don't want you getting hurt by some shitbird who has no feelings for you. You're right though: it's your decision, not ours."

I wanted to keep the conversation focused on the identity of my father so I didn't comment on his absence from my life. Instead I asked, "If you don't know who he is, does that mean he could be Maynard Bandy?"

"It ain't Maynard," J.T. said.

"How do you know, Granddad? How can you be sure?"

"Your mother told us it wasn't Maynard and I checked. He was in jail when she got pregnant."

"But I'm carrying his name, for Pete's sake! Why was I told repeatedly that he was my father if he wasn't?"

Ella jumped into the discussion wiping a tear away. "I want to explain it, J.T., because it was my idea. Rupe, baby, please listen to me with an open mind. You don't remember this, but twenty-five years ago on this little island, illegitimate children and unwed mothers were not welcome. They were ridiculed and often run out of town."

"I had a classmate named Delores Rhody, Rupe," J.T. interceded. "We were in the same elementary and junior high classes so I knew her well. She got pregnant in the ninth grade, left a pathetic little note, and hanged herself in her backyard. Mazie was depressed when she got pregnant and she had something called anxiety disorder. The doctor told us it was a worrisome combination. We watched her very closely for months because we thought she might do what Delores did," J.T. said.

"We figured the best way we had of preserving

Vendetta

Mazie's reputation was to make sure her husband believed he was the father. If Maynard had doubts – and he was a distrustful soul – others would too. And, if rumors started, we feared she might take you and run away, or take her own life." Ella paused, bit her bottom lip. "She and I talked it out right here at this table. I told her, 'Honeychild, if you still have kindly feelings toward Maynard, spending a night with him might be a damned sight better than hearing ugly comments about your baby for a long time to come.'" J.T. reached over and took Ella's hand, hoping she would stop, but she couldn't yet. "I didn't need to know they went to the Southernmost Motel, but I sure felt better when she told me Maynard was pleased to be a father. I'm ashamed too, Rupe, for what I suggested, I really am. But to be absolutely honest, you know, I would have done worse things to protect you and Mazie from humiliation and shame."

"Jesus God," was all I could say. We all sat avoiding eye contact for a spell, but there was more business to attend to so I pressed on. "Okay," I get it," I said, "but why did she refuse to tell me who my father is. Why? I don't get it."

"I've thought about that question every day," J.T. said. "I believe it boils down to two possibilities: shame or fear. My little girl was either so ashamed of what she did or so afraid of what the father would do if she divulged his name that she went to her Maker protecting that secret." J.T. swallowed hard. "I'm an old fart now, but I ain't dead and I'd love to have ten minutes alone with that bastard."

Ella did not take the bait but shot him a nasty glance. The old vendetta argument was still alive. "Rupe, my love," she said standing up, "we have tried to do our best for you all your life. I hope you won't judge us based on this one decision." She looked at me

16

and opened her arms. I walked to her and she folded them around me. That night I went to B.O.'s Fishwagon, a ramshackle bar on the water, and had a beer or two more than usual.

~ ~ ~

J.T. and Ella left on vacation the following day. I told them I would spend the nights there for safety sake until they returned. My first night there, as I headed for a cold beer after work, I found a note from Bea on the kitchen counter. It said,

"R, gotta see you sometime. Pls call. Love, B."

I called her right away and said, "I have excellent leftovers. Come on over."

At fifty-two, Bea had a trim figure, played excellent tennis, and looked ten years younger than her age. But that evening when she walked into the kitchen with a bottle of chilled wine, she looked at least her age and was obviously preoccupied.

"What's up, Beatrice?" I asked giving her a peck on the cheek.

"Let's eat first," she said. We heated the leftovers and had a couple glasses of wine, but she did not eat much. I was still processing the information from J.T. and Ella, but I felt relieved to know the secret that had been lodged between them and me for so long was out in the open. The healing could begin, I thought. Little did I know.

"I have some information for you," Bea said tentatively.

"About what?"

"About your father." She read the expression on my face and said, "Sorry, Rupe. I've been so nervous about this moment. I didn't know how to begin."

"What's the info?" I asked, trying to act calm. Still she hesitated.

"Look," I continued, "you know better than anyone

in the world how often I have wondered who he is, what he's like, what I'd be like if he'd been around. Please, Bea."

"Okay, here goes." She took a deep breath. "When you were about eleven I took your mother to Miami to buy a car and you came with us. Maybe you remember that trip."

"Yes, I remember it," I said, nodding.

Bea reminded me that she dropped Mazie and me at the car dealership, and set out to visit a friend, but as she drove away her conscience began to bother her. "It kept whispering in my ear, 'Don't leave Rupe,' she said. So, she returned to the dealership, arriving with almost an hour before she was to meet us for lunch. To pass the time, she sat in the grand showroom; she looked at the shiny new Ford models on display; she wandered the lots outside, all the time keeping an eye out for us. When she didn't see us, Bea said, she began to feel vaguely uneasy about me. Then, in front of the corporate offices, she spotted a trophy wall laden with newspaper articles, photos, and memorabilia. As she scanned the material, her eyes happened upon a photo of two men shaking hands. She read the caption: "Movie Director Quentin Tarantino and Miami Film Studios President Mr. E. Rupert Shifflet discuss a venture at the Fontainebleau Hotel."

"Oh, shit!" I said aloud. It was my worst nightmare, and yet I was awake, sitting in my grandparents' kitchen. Bea had stopped talking. She was looking at me.

"It's Earl Shifflet?" I asked in a whisper.

She nodded. We sat and stared at each other. "I'm sorry, Rupe," she said at last. "When I saw that middle name..."

"Me too," I interrupted. "It was like an explosion in my head."

"Yeah, the middle name and the movie studio. I had no idea Shifflet had a movie studio but ... sonofabitch." Suddenly tears of rage were running down Bea's cheeks and her face was turning red. I reached out and put my hand on hers. I felt my face go warm too as a volcano of anger welled up in me.

"Are you absolutely positive about this, Bea?"

"I'm sure. I invited Mazie to dinner the next night and she confirmed my fears."

"How did she react when you said his name? I asked.

"She was frightened, really scared!"

"Why was that?"

"Because she thought Shifflet might kill you – and her. Remember, Mazie was only seventeen then when you were born. If his affair with a minor had been discovered, he could have been prosecuted for statutory rape, consensual or not. Imagine how much more difficult it would have been to prosecute that case if you and Mazie were dead."

"No wonder she never told anybody," I said, aghast.

"Except me," Bea pointed out. "She considered it safer to tell me everything so I would appreciate the danger and keep the secret rather than to keep me in the dark and risk my talking about it.

"But she fell for such a jerk!"

"She was an impressionable teenager, my dear, and he treated her well," Bea explained, instinctively defending her little sister. "He took her to popular night spots, provided her an apartment on South Beach, and talked of making her a movie star. I asked her outright if she knew of Shifflet's reputation and she said, 'No idea, Sister! I was seventeen! What would I know about vice and corruption?' She thought his only business was the film studio," Bea said. Bea thought for a moment. "You know, she spoke of Shifflet as if she really liked him – and probably was naïve enough to think he actually had some affection for her – until she told him she was pregnant."

"Why? What did he do then?"

"He turned on her like the animal he is. She told me he hit her and knocked her to the floor. Gave her a gash on the head that needed stitches. Then he whispered in her ear, 'You are dead to me, Bitch, and your baby is dead too if you ever breathe a word of this to anyone ... and I'll know it if you do.' Then he yelled, 'Get out!' Now you know why she didn't tell Daddy, right? Can you imagine what he would have done if he'd heard about that little tantrum?" Bea asked.

"Yeah, I can imagine alright," I said absentmindedly, but my thoughts were carrying me back to my own horrendous morning with Shifflet. I had kept those memories locked away, but they broke out when I heard what he did to Mama. I remembered the hand on me, the sickeningly sweet smell of his aftershave, his grimace, and then I thought of my mother..."

"This goes to show you his temper and how dangerous he is." Bea was saying. "I know this must just fill you with rage, Rupe...

"No you don't!" I cut her off and stood, aware that my voice didn't sound like mine. "You don't have any idea how it makes me feel." Bea starred at me. "That bastard molested me when I was eleven years old ... when we went up there together." I felt faint so I bent over and put my hands on my knees. "He said I'd be dead if I told anyone." Bea came over and put her hand on my back.

"Oh, my God! I'm so sorry, Rupie," she said several times. "I'm so sorry I didn't notice you had been hurt ... didn't do anything to help you understand it wasn't your fault." An instant later, she screamed violently at her anger. I reached out and took her wrists. She tried to tear herself away from me, but I held onto her for fear she would injure herself. I held tightly to her wrists and tried to reassure her gently until the tantrum passed. When it did, I turned her loose and sat down next to her shaking and sweaty. It seemed like several minutes passed before either of us spoke.

"We'll find a good counselor for you to talk to if you want some professional guidance," she said calmly. "Anything you want, Rupie," she said. "Anything."

"Are you okay?" I asked.

"No, I am filled with hatred now, but your secret is safe with me and my best advice: "Let's you and me keep it as safe as your Mama did."

My own father had molested me. Jesus! There was so much to think about I didn't know where to start. Bea offered to stay the night, but I wanted to be alone. I needed solitude to clear my head. I walked her home along the quiet sidewalks, asked her if she wanted me to stay with her, and gave her a hug. When I returned, I was tempted to pour myself a shot or two of J.T.'s Laphroaig Scotch, but I collapsed instead onto a lounge chair on the dock and lay there exhausted, listening to the music of the mini-waves lapping on shore and savoring the touch of the soft, tropical air.

As I lay there and felt the stress slightly loosen its grip on my neck and shoulders, I realized my mind had been working on its own: Mama had been right to keep the truth about Earl Shifflet from me. She had been right also to keep his identity a secret – even to the point of taking it to her grave. Earl Shifflet was a psychopath and Mama had sacrificed a normal life and much more to shelter me from him. I owed her so much for that. I owed her revenge.

I was so exhausted that these dark thoughts blew

away like smoke on a windy day as soon as my head hit the pillow. I awoke at 7 a.m. with those same thoughts eating their way into my conscience, but I had to go to work. J.T. put me in charge, at least nominally, when he was gone. While waiting for my coffee at the Five Brothers, I had an epiphany: I could not discuss this with anyone. If I did and were charged with murder later, anyone who had discussed it with me could be found guilty of conspiracy to commit murder. I was alone, contemplating murder, a circumstance so alien to me I felt as if I had drifted outside myself.

~ ~ ~

I met J.T. and Ella at the airport that afternoon and before they had put their bags in the trunk Ella said, "Rupie, you look tired. Are you okay?"

"One hundred percent," I said, although that was far from the truth. In fact, I was stymied. I had been thinking about striking back at Shifflet throughout their vacation, but had come up with no workable ideas, much less a plan. I had discarded the thought of going to the police because I couldn't envision how a case could be made against him. His offenses against Mazie and me occurred without witnesses and long ago. Only the effects of his repulsive deeds remained raw and current.

I had visited Shifflet's dealership while they were away, hoping to learn or see something there that would spark my imagination. The salesman who greeted me was a garrulous fellow so I was able to divert our conversation temporarily from my alleged need for a car to his job and then to Shifflet. "Do you want to meet him," he asked enthusiastically. "He likes to meet customers. He's here today – just saw him."

"No, no. I don't have much time this morning." I said. "Next time maybe. He's got quite a reputation."

"Yeah, I've heard all the rumors," the salesman

said. "Tell you what, if you buy a car from me, I'll introduce him to you. You can ask him about his reputation yourself," he said with a wink. Eventually he got down to business and tried to sell me a car and I tried to appear interested but not quite ready to buy. I asked for his card and promised I'd contact him soon.

The salesman's offer to introduce me to Shifflet made me face the fact that I could probably get close enough to shoot him. The question was: if I were close enough to shoot, would I? Could I gun this monster down in cold blood? The moment of truth was drawing near.

The next day I went for a swim after work, as usual. I dove off the dock, swam underwater as far as I could. As I broke the surface and sucked in that first lung-full of sweet sea air I knew I could not kill him. I knew revenge would not be sweet enough to warrant betting my wonderful life against death in the gas chamber, and I knew that my life for his would be a stupid exchange. Maybe I had known these things all along and had denied them because I wanted so much to make that man pay for all the years he made Mama suffer. Maybe I denied them because deep down I wanted to show I was as brave as my grandfather had been during the war. But, I knew that evening as I swam back to the dock that I was not my grandfather and the two situations were far from equivalent.

Having acknowledged that I could not kill Shifflet myself, I found I couldn't just dump this mess in J.T.'s lap either. He was almost seventy, had a bad leg and a heart problem he didn't talk about. If I told him what Shifflet had done to Mazie and me, it would have been the same as urging him to go out and get even for us. His pride would have compelled him to try, and in doing so, he would have been risking the good life he had built for himself and all of his family and all of our futures. The final answer was clear: Shifflet was not worth any risk to our family.

And so I found myself in the same position my Mama had been in: Shifflet's threat to kill me followed me around like the menace of a bad disease, but I was neither willing nor able to eliminate that threat. Just like my Mama had been, I was frustrated, even shamed by our bad luck, and yet we had each decided to live with it because we realized it was better than the alternatives.

~ ~ ~

I awoke in my own bedroom that unforgettable morning fifty years ago to the coos of mourning doves and the rustling of palm fronds. I padded to the kitchen to make my Cuban *café con leche*. Bea usually made our coffee while she puttered in the kitchen in the early morning, but she had left a note for me the previous afternoon saying she was going to babysit Kat Dannenberg, her goddaughter, and might spend the night there if her parents stayed out late. With her note in hand and clad only in my boxer shorts, I went out the front door and down the porch steps to retrieve the *Miami Herald* from under the jasmine hedge. I slipped it out of its plastic sleeve, unfolded it, and stood suddenly paralyzed by the headline: "Mob Boss Slain At Home."

I stared at a gruesome picture of Shifflet's body splayed out on a flagstone path in his front yard. I don't think I moved again until I finished reading the three-column article. It sounded as if it were written by an experienced homicide reporter who, based on the trajectories of the fatal .45-caliber slugs, suggested Shifflet had been "assassinated by a professional." One bullet had entered at the top right side of his skull, plowed across both hemispheres of the brain and exited his ear. The other had entered the back of his head and exited the windpipe. The obituary described Shifflet as "a shadowy figure," who had been implicated, but never prosecuted, in two mob slayings and was known to have been close to Medellin drug lord Pablo Escobar in the 1980's.

When my mind returned to the present, I thought of Bea, the only person who knew of my connection to Shifflet, so I grabbed the phone and called the Dannenbergs. Rob answered.

"She's not here, Rupe."

"Did she babysit for Kat last night?" I asked.

"Nope. She babysat Thursday, night before last, so we could play *bocce*. Is everything okay?"

"Oh yeah. No problem. I guess I confused one night for the other."

Bea walked in the front door thirty minutes later.

"Hey, good morning, Beatrice," I said. "You got an early start today!"

"Didn't you see my note?"

"No," I lied spontaneously. I had never lied to Bea. I was shocked that I had just done so, but I had just begun to think the unthinkable and I knew, as one knows in a chess match, that her next move, her answer, could checkmate her. I felt sick with anxiety as I endured that interminable second before she replied.

"I've been at the Dannenbergs," she said, and my heart sank. "Stayed over because they got home so late." I believed Bea had never lied to me either and she didn't do it well. She looked at me, but only briefly. The color drained from her face. "I've got to freshen up and you have to go to the Marina, don't you?"

"Have you seen the *Herald* today?" I asked. "You should check out the front page before you freshen up." I gestured at the paper on the kitchen table and suddenly felt great sympathy for her. She knew what was coming. She placed her hands palms down on the table on either side of the paper, a four-point stance to steady herself, and bent over it so her head was directly above the headline and a photo of Shifflet. She looked at it, closed her eyes, and gasped. Her legs gave out just as I reached her side and helped her to the sofa. I sat next to her, held her hand, and waited for her to regain control. Finally she sighed deeply and said, "It was so easy to do."

"Shhhhh. It's just you and me, Bea. No one else will ever know."

Mr. Crane's New Paintings

Brewster Chamberlin

It was 10:30 on a hot spring morning and the dark interior of The Edge Bar in Key West provided a cool and soothing haven from the climate. The blonde bartender eyed the only two customers in the place, his leg muscles tense and his hands resting lightly on the bar. He did not expect the necessity would arise, but he liked to be prepared.

Mrs. Crane leaned her left elbow carefully on the dark wood and with equal care pronounced, "If you do not leave this place immediately, you will experience a vast amount of pain." Her voice carried the conviction of someone entirely sure that whatever she said would in fact happen.

This assurance baffled the drunken tourist in the pale green Bermuda shorts standing too close to her. He blinked gritty eyelids rapidly in confusion and burped whiskey fumes into the air. He plastered what he considered to be an affable grin on his face, a gesture that almost always won him some time from the victims of his transparent attentions.

"Aw, now, listen, snooks, whyn't we move up to my room in that fine little hotel across the street and mambo, hey?" As he talked he moved forward slightly and moved his hand toward her arm so that it came as a complete surprise to find himself on the unswept floor clutching his groin in breath-stopping agony.

The bartender walked slowly around the edge of

the mahogany, shaking his head. He lifted the gasping tourist to his feet and propelled him gently through the batwing doors to the street corner. He sat the moaning drunk on the city bench and came back into the saloon.

"It's always a pleasure to watch you work, Cora," he said wiping the bar with a pristine white cloth, "a true pleasure."

"Hershel, my name is not Cora and that wasn't work, but rather an unfortunate and sad necessity."

"I know, Mrs. Crane, but sometimes I can't resist."

"If you'd control your customers the way you do the whiskey, this wouldn't happen."

"Business is business, Mrs. C. And who coulda told he was that type of drunk. Not all bartenders are crystal ball readers. He shoulda stayed in Sloppy Joes where his type belongs."

"An asshole, Hershel, as anyone could have seen from his pants."

"Books by their covers, Mrs. C., and tourists by their clothes, but here's Mr. C. himself with a new haircut – by which you can't tell anything about him except where he comes from. Hello, Mr. Crane, who's going to take the election?"

"Ike for another four, Hershel, no doubt about it. Just what the country needs."

"The country doesn't need his fascist partner," Mrs. Crane said flatly.

"Now, Cora, you might control these expressions of your inexplicable pinkish politics," Mr. Crane admonished.

"The usual, Mr. C.?" asked the bartender who had heard them at it before.

"Too early for me, Hershel. A cool glass of refreshing mineral water, if you please. Mrs. Crane holds her liquor better than I do at this hour. It's her politics that are out of control – or is it 'is' out of control?"

28

"Here you are, club soda with one ice cube and no lime slice. Bottoms up. And my name is Steve, by the way. As you very well know. I whistle very well indeed."

"We're well aware of that, Hershel," Mrs. Crane said with a smile, "but you'll always be Hershel to us."

"*L'chaim,*" the bartender replied with a shrug and a toss of his long blonde hair. Mr. Crane admired the hair but not the gesture, which he considered too baroque for the time and place. On the other hand, Mrs. Crane was only Cora in bars before noon.

Finishing his club soda, Mr. Crane said, "We must be off, my dear." He turned to the bartender. "An appointment at the Navy Yard."

"Another portrait?"

"I certainly hope so."

"Yes, otherwise we won't be able to afford these watered down drinks," Mrs. Crane said warmly.

"Ice melts, Cora." The bartender grinned. "Can't do much about that, not in this weather."

"So long, Hershel."

Outside on the street Mr. Crane put on sunglasses and said, "If you'd dress less whorishly, you'd probably avoid these things. Hershel's too much a gentleman to tell you that."

"But how boring life would be."

Mr. Crane smiled at his wife and they walked toward the base. "Yes," he said, "I guess it would be."

"And the Admiral likes it. Do you really have a portrait commission?"

"I certainly hope not. Lord, I hate painting these stuffed shirts."

"The great protectors of the nation's waters."

"I'd rather do the sailors; they're more interesting."

"But they can't pay your rates and can't get you in to see the admirals, which is the whole point of the legend, isn't it? Portrait painter has unquestioned access to admirals on the base, and so forth."

"Especially accompanied by his whorish looking wife."

"Exactly."

"Sometimes I think I should have stayed with the agency. This contract work is too unpredictable."

"You really had no alternative, did you? Mr. Fall Guy. What a horrid set up."

"Anyway, I think I'll stop accepting assignments."

"And whorish wife can work the street to pay the bills."

"Too old and tired. Want to retire to a deserted island and paint pictures of sea birds."

"This island is deserted enough in the summer."

"Not far enough away from Washington."

"No place is."

"Here we are. Now smile at the guard while I show my sketch pad and invitation letter."

The guard asked them to wait under the palm trees at the side of the white sentry box. In a few minutes a young officer came to escort them to the Admiral's office in a non-descript gray waterfront building. Each time they came, a different young officer performed this duty: the Admiral spread the perks among his staff as well as he could. This ensign had trouble focusing his eyes on the hallways and whistled an erratic tune in his head. Mr. Crane sympathized and knew precisely what the young man would say to his fellow junior officers at the mess that afternoon. Mrs. Crane had that effect on men and women of all ages and genders, not excepting Mr. Crane himself.

The Admiral allowed himself the indulgence of enjoying the effect, but long years at sea in command had given him great powers of discipline. His office reflected the austere character of its inhabitant with not an extraneous item in the room except a two-feet long model of the battleship *Maine* on a polished oak stand bearing the phrase "Know your enemy and you will not be surprised." A recent model air conditioner loudly chugged away in the room's single window. Even if a microphone bug could have been planted in the room, a listener could hear only the machine's motor and a garbled babble of voices.

His gray eyes sparkled as he welcomed them and indicted the straight-back wood chairs. "*Always* a pleasure to see you, Mrs. Crane."

"And you, too, Admiral. You're looking devilishly well."

"Good of you to say that." The Admiral smiled and tugged his uniform jacket by its hem. "I must admit I feel well. Better since I stopped smoking. No, you go ahead, the air conditioner seems to ventilate the smoke."

The Cranes lit up Old Golds and waited for the assignment.

As always, the Admiral went directly to the point. "We have a problem with one of the civilian employees you might be able to help us resolve. No travel this time."

"A shame. Visiting Alaska at this point would be a cool thing to do," Mrs. Crane said wistfully.

"Assuredly, my dear, but not on this time. *Tant pis pour vous, tant mieux pour nous*, or in any case less expensive."

The Admiral smiled and Mr. Crane returned the gesture.

"Admiral, I always admire your level of achievement. How did you ever last in the military?"

"Camouflage, Mr. Crane, and I've been seconded to this *civilian* agency for several years now."

"Deep cover, eh?"

"Carefully constructed legend, indeed."

"Even Boston or Stockholm would be nice," Mrs. Crane said wistfully.

"Didn't think you'd want to go back to Sweden, my dear," the Admiral said.

"That was a long time ago. I've forgotten all about it by now."

Mr. Crane knew this was not true and hastened to bring their attention back to the subject. "What is the local problem Navy security can't handle?"

"We don't want them to know that there is a problem. That would be embarrassing for everyone." The Admiral's gray eyes grew cold and he continued in a thin voice, "This must be handled outside the normal channels. With the correctly gauged pressure, the issue will go away on its own, before it becomes an official matter."

"Blackmail, Admiral?" Mr. Crane said with a smile.

"It may come to that, but can have no connection to the man's job, of course."

"Of course."

"I am somewhat at a loss, though I get the drift of your opaque conversation," Mrs. Crane protested. "What exactly is the problem?"

"We have reason to believe this fellow is passing or is planning to pass highly classified information to the Cubans," the Admiral said and waited for the inevitable reaction.

Mr. Crane shook his head and Mrs. Crane laughed out loud. "Admiral," she said with a sense of wonder in her voice, "Admiral, Cuba is an ally in the great crusade. We *own* Havana, or at least the Italians in New York do. What ...?"

"Yes, of course. Your reaction was expected and I admit with a small sense of smug satisfaction that I played to it. Nonetheless, the matter is of deep seriousness, and could play into the hands of our enemies in Cuba and in Moscow." The Admiral took a short breath. "Let me explain."

"Please do already," Mr. Crane grinned.

"You will see, I think, how serious this matter is. Washington is quite upset about the Negative Possibilities." Mr. Crane removed the grin from his face and nodded with the appropriate solemnity. Mrs. Crane looked blankly at the Admiral. "You know that planners in the agency and the military are charged with the preparation of a wide variety of contingency plans for even the most improbably situations. The invasion and occupation of Cuba is one of the more improbable of these contingencies." The Admiral sniffed in the chilled, conditioned air. "Why we would even want to implement such a plan is beyond me. Batista is a somctimes uncomfortable but steady anti-communist ally."

"He's a fascist dictator of a police state whose own people would love to get rid of," Mrs. Crane pronounced, crossing her legs for emphasis.

"As I said, he is a faithful anti-red ally and guards the southern perimeter of the eastern United States."

"Along with our forces at Guantánamo, and here," Mr. Crane added.

"Yes, of course. My point is that we have reason to believe one of the civilians on the base with access to information about this contingency plan is about to give or sell it to the Cubans. We want you to see to it that this does not happen."

"How do we know what he intends to do if he hasn't done it yet?" Mr. Crane said.

"His boy friend is a very patriotic, if sexually warped, young man, who also works on the base as a driver for the base commander. When Jack Wood, the suspect, began to hang out in the Cuban joints along Duval and spend time at the San Carlos Institute, the boy friend became suspicious."

"Why?" Mrs. Crane said.

"Jack Wood hates Cuban food," the Admiral stated flatly.

"Ah, of course. Very suspicious behavior," Mrs. Crane agreed.

"Indeed. The boy friend brought that matter to the attention of the intelligence ops on the base who fortunately came to my staff with it."

"Shouldn't the FBI normally deal with this," Mr. Crane put it tentatively. "Even if Jack Wood is planning a trip to Havana, it's a domestic matter."

"Hoover is an incompetent pervert whose only talent is the manipulation of the system for his own survival. We have it on the Highest Authority that it is the agency's responsibility, not the FBI's." The Admiral blew his nose and allowed the blood that had suffused his face to subside. "Although this pattern of abnormal behavior – I mean his sudden interest in things Cuban, not his perverted sexual interests – is not in itself sufficient to alarm us, the fact that one of the man's main work tasks is to constantly update the Cuban contingency plan, coupled with this new interest is very alarming indeed. Your job is to see to it that he does not carry out his intention, or if he has already started it to stop it."

"If in fact it is his intention."

"Of course. We've compiled a brief file on his history for you. Speed obviously is of the essence."

Mrs. Crane looked doubtful and re-crossed her legs and leaned forward to please the Admiral. "Homosexuality is still cause for dismissal, isn't it? Didn't the security clearance process show up his sexual inclinations?"

"The process in this case lacked comprehensiveness," the Admiral said with grim determination. "Needless to say we did not conduct it." He forced his eyes away from Mrs. Crane's summer cleavage. "The sooner you resolve this, the better."

The Cranes took their leave to begin the assignment. The Admiral's eyes followed Mrs. Crane's undulations out the door. As it closed he sighed briefly before turning his attention to the next project.

In the final analysis, the denouement turned out to be fairly easily arranged; it was almost an anticlimax to the story. As Mr. Crane said later, lifting his scotch highball in mock tribute, "Weak humans are generally predictable. All you have to do is play to their weakness and you've got them. Sometimes they act irrationally, but generally they are perfectly predictable."

Mr. Crane, however, did not like himself much for several weeks after he'd completed the assignment and he painted terrible canvases of distorted human bodies in impossible positions using garish primary colors. Later still, he destroyed all but one of the paintings. This one he stored in the crawl space above the living room in the conch house where he and Mrs. Crane lived in almost complete anonymity.

He had brought the Cuban boy and the photographer down from Miami and it took less than a week to do the job. Three days afterward Jack Wood resigned his position with the Navy and moved to Savannah where he drowned himself in the river a week later. He had passed no information to the Cubans that anyone could discover.

Mr. Crane worked very hard at the colorful grotesque paintings and did not go to see the Admiral to be congratulated on a successful mission. Mrs. Crane went more frequently to The Edge Bar during these weeks, but only once did the bartender have the opportunity to tell her how much he appreciated her work.

35

Four Fingers and the Watch Fob

Shirrel Rhoades

Wharton "Four Fingers" Dalessandro was having a Red Stripe at Schooner Wharf. His pal Dunk Reid hadn't shown up today for their chess game. They always set up the board on a small table out on the rough weathered planks that lined the Key West Bight. Evalena let them store the table and two folding chairs in a back corner of the bar. She was major domo of Schooner Wharf, the seaport bar and restaurant with the motto "Hanging With the Big Dogs." You could always find more tourists than big dogs; but quite a few locals blended among the patrons for beers and hot wings and fried shrimp.

Ever since cashiering out of NYPD some 17 years ago, thanks to a stray bullet, Dalessandro had lived a frugal life here in Key West, painting houses now and then for beer money, playing chess most days with Dunk.

His nickname – Four Fingers – came from a missing digit on his right hand, nothing to do with his previous life as a cop, but the result of a fishing accident in the Dry Tortugas. Damn, sometimes he missed that finger.

Funny that Dunk hadn't left a message with the bartender. Wasn't like him to leave Four Fingers hanging.

"Hey, didja hear? Dunk Reid's been arrested for murder!" announced Paul Macaw as he took the stage. The singer was filling in as today's entertainment. Headliner Michael McCloud had a head cold that made his voice sound like a bullfrog.

"No way," said a fat man at a table in the front of the stage. "Dunk Reid wouldn't hurt a fly."

"How 'bout the fly on his pants?" shouted a fisherman in back. "He's always unzipping it at the sight of a pretty woman."

True enough, Dunk had a reputation as a ladies' man, always taking cute tourists out on his boat. "Fishing," he called it. No one was quite sure what he used as bait. But fact is, the Conch was a trust fund baby, with a steady income from the wad of money that had been left to him by his daddy, a successful sponger.

Four Fingers stood up and took a step in the direction of the stage. "Dunk's been arrested?"

"You betcha. Police Chief Johnny Leigh put the cuffs on him as he docked his boat earlier today at the Yacht Club." Dunk owned a 38-foot fishing boat that was similar to Hemingway's *Pilar*. Dunk had named his boat *Pillow*. It was a floating bedroom.

"Who'd he supposedly kill?" shouted Four Fingers over the din of the crowd. Tourists were getting restless for Paul Macaw to start his set, sing his popular song, "Sittin' Here in Key West Without a Dime to My Name." Contrary to the song's title, Paul was a millionaire from winning the Florida Lottery. First thing, he'd bought a boat bigger than Dunk's.

"Some tourist gal. A cute redhead. They found her body out on Christmas Tree Island, strangled with Dunk's watch chain."

"How did they know it was Dunk's chain?"

"Cause it still had his watch on one end of it. Inside

38

the lid it's engraved: 'To Dunk from Louise.'"

"Oh."

Just then Police Chief Johnny Leigh walked into the open-air bar, flanked by two of his deputies. "Dalessandro, there you are. Come with us," he motioned to Four Fingers.

"What? You want to arrest me too?"

The Chief looked puzzled. "Why would we want to do that? I just need your help interviewing Dunk Reid. I figure he'll talk to you, his ol' chess buddy. He won't say a word to us."

"Probably ticked off with you for arresting him."

The young lawman frowned. He was a handsome Hispanic, skin as smooth as caramel. "Didn't have much choice. We found a dead tourist. She'd been strangled with Dunk's watch fob."

"So I heard from Paul here. But you know he didn't do it, don't you?"

"What makes you say that?" Johnny Leigh sometimes used Four Fingers to help him solve a crime. He knew the former New York City cop had a knack for figuring out murders in four minutes or less. He'd been clocked with a stopwatch on more than one occasion.

Four Fingers stepped closer, eye-to-eye with the police chief. "First of all, Dunk's ex-wife was a hot-headed carrot top. It wasn't a pretty divorce. Paul here says the dead tourist was a redhead. I'm pretty sure Dunk would never go out with another redhead."

Johnny Leigh said, "I didn't know Dunk had been married before."

"In his younger days. He doesn't like to talk about it. But it certainly soured him on redheads."

"Then how do you explain his fob around her neck?" The crowd at the Schooner Wharf was taking in this exchange, having forgotten about Paul Macaw singing "Sittin' Here in Key West Without a Dime to My

Name."

The performer returned his guitar to its case, stepped off the stage to join the police chief and Four Fingers. "Yeah, that proves Dunk done it," he said.

"Somebody stole Dunk's pocket watch and chain a few days ago," said Four Fingers. "He told me it was missing."

"Who'd steal that crappy old watch? It barely kept time," said Paul Macaw.

"Pretty sure you did," said Four Fingers. "You used to be a pick pocket working Mallory Square before you took up entertaining."

"That's right, Paul. You've got quite an arrest records," nodded the police chief. "I've pulled you in a few times myself."

"Why would I steal a cheap watch? I won the Lottery last year. I'm richer'n King Croesus."

"Old habits die hard," shrugged Four Fingers. "Maybe you just like keeping your hand in."

"You can't prove any of that."

"Sure, I can. When you told me about the dead girl, you mentioned that the watch was engraved 'To Dunk from Louise.'"

"Yeah, so what?"

"Only person who would know that is the person who stole the watch," Four Fingers pointed out. "Louise Lowe was the name of Dunk's wife; she gave him the watch. He was embarrassed by that youthful misstep of marrying Louise, so he never let anybody see that engraved message. I only know about it because I once won it off him betting on a chess game. He eventually won it back and made me promise never to tell. But I guess these circumstances oughta release me from my word."

"Paul, if you had the watch and chain, that means you killed that tourist girl," stated Johnny Leigh, motioning for his deputies to take custody of the singer.

"That's crazy."

"People say you like to pick up tourist girls and take them on a romantic cruise," said Four Fingers. "I hear you like to anchor off Christmas Tree Island."

"Why would I kill that girl Wanda? I don't have a motive."

"You can stop right there," said the police chief. "You just put the nail in your coffin when you called the girl Wanda. We haven't released the victim's name yet. So how did you know it if –?"

"Okay, okay, you got me. I killed that little redheaded bitch. She tried to back out and things got out of hand. Never should have left that watch and chain behind. It was in my pocket and I wrapped it around her neck and pulled on it till her eyes bulged like a frog's. She deserved it for being so standoffish."

"Take him away, boys," growled the police chief. "Make sure you read him his rights." The crowd cheered as the deputies hustled away their prisoner. There would be no performance of "Sittin' Here in Key West Without a Dime to My Name" today.

"Johnny –" said Four Fingers.

"Yeah, Dalessandro, what is it?"

"Could you please phone the station and tell your minions to release Dunk. If the rascal hurries, he can get down here in time for a game of chess before the sun sets."

The Duchess

Andrew Daly

Per someone (Waugh I believe), the perfect short story has to include sex, royalty and religion:

Oh my God, said the Duchess, how could a dead man afford Key West?

The Sunset Slasher

Bill Craig

June 10th, Key West.

Mallory Square was crowded as sunset drew closer. Little did anyone know that a monster had landed in paradise. He walked anonymously among them, just another face in the crowd. It wouldn't be until later, after night had fallen that his presence would be revealed. My name is Harry Dove and I'm a stringer for the Independent News Service covering the Florida Keys in general and Key West in particular. Mostly I worked from home after having a career that had taken me around to world to exotic locations before I decided I was tired of the cold up north and getting shot at in countries whose languages I didn't speak.

I was on the square that evening as well, watching the street performers juggling fire and doing assorted tricks and acts for the tourists. After the sunset, I retired to Pepe's for a cold adult beverage and the company of an old friend named Thom Hark who worked for the local rag, *The Key West Citizen*.

"Harry Dove, you old sod, when did you get back to town? Weren't you up in Miami covering the Santorini trial?" Hark asked, taking a swig from his bottle of Budweiser.

"I was, but once he got convicted the story was over so I came home," I replied. Like all newspapermen, Thom could be really inquisitive.

"Always after the story, eh Harry? Even at our age?"

"We may be old, Thom, but we aren't dead. You

know me, as long as there is a story I'll chase it."

"To the chase," Hark raised his bottle and I raised mine, clinking them together.

"Anything been shaking down here while I've been out of town?" I asked.

"I should make you read the paper like everyone else, but I do owe you one. A young woman was found murdered a couple of nights ago behind the Green Parrot. Her throat had been cut and so far, the police have no suspects," Hark told me in conspiratorial whisper.

"Really? Are you covering it for the *Citizen*?" I asked.

"My beat has more to do with local politics these days."

"That wasn't a no."

"But it wasn't a yes, either, my friend. In other words, Harry, do your own bloody legwork. I shared what I knew, anything else is on you."

"Good enough, Thom," I grinned, but my mind was racing. A girl murdered behind the Parrot. Was she a local or a tourist? How much coverage had the story got so far? And more importantly, had it hit the wire services yet?

"I'm getting ready to move along to the Smokin' Tuna. Haskins is supposed to be there along with that Fed, Dan Burger."

"Haskins is running around with a Fed? Why?"

"Old friends I suppose. Of course, he might be in town for a different reason." Hark had a mischievous look in his eye. He had me hooked and he knew it. We paid our tab and headed over to Duval Street. Night had settled in now but you couldn't tell it from the huge throngs of people wandering around from bar to bar and shop to shop. The air was balmy, but there was a cool breeze blowing and the humidity was lower than normal. We only had worked up a mild sweat by the time we passed the Red Garter and turned down Charles Street where the Smokin' Tuna sat hidden at the back of the street.

We were almost to the entrance to the Tuna when a horrible shriek rang out from behind the building. For a newspaperman, it was the clarion call to battle and Thom and I raced around the corner. What we witnessed brought us both up short. A tall thin man was slashing a blade across the throat of a young woman who was already bleeding from several other wounds. "Stop!" Thom's voice rang out as I lifted my digital camera and started snapping pictures. Based on the amount of blood on the ground around her, the girl was already gone. The man with the knife growled at us and then fled off into the darkness as people began pouring around the corner and out the back door to see what was going on. Someone had pulled out a cell phone and dialed 911. I popped the memory card from my camera and slipped it into a pocket, replacing it with an empty one. I began snapping more pictures of both the body and of the crowd on the off chance that the killer had doubled back.

From what I had seen of his face that didn't seem likely but I've been wrong before. There had been something truly horrific in what I had seen of his face, and I knew it would probably haunt my nightmares if I was even able to sleep this night. Over the years, I had seen a lot of things, not all of them easily explained, and yes, those still haunt me when I close my eyes. But that is a story for another time.

It didn't take long for the cops to arrive to break up the crowd and start securing the scene. Thom and I both were detained because we were eyewitnesses to the end of the attack, the part that had certainly been fatal. We were separated and isolated so that we couldn't compare notes on what we had seen, standard operation procedure for the cops.

It took about twenty minutes for the detectives to arrive. Ernesto Ortiz and Raul Quintana. I had almost hoped that Chief Gutierrez had come along because I knew him. I hadn't met either of these two before.

By luck of the draw I got Ortiz and he was a younger man, less cynical than his partner who was in the back of the other car talking to Thom Hark. "Okay, tell me what you saw?" Ortiz ordered.

"My friend and I heard a scream, ran around back, saw a tall, thin guy in dark clothes slashing the dead woman's throat. My friend yelled for him to stop and he turned around and growled at us, then ran off. I started taking pictures, but he was already gone," I explained. I made sure not to mention that I had gotten at least one good shot of his face before switching memory cards. That might come in handy later.

"Your camera digital?" Ortiz asked.

"It is," I acknowledged.

"Hand over the memory card," Ortiz extended his hand. I decided to be reasonable and hand it over.

"I work for the Independent New Service. I'm a reporter, Harry Dove."

"I know who you are, Mr. Dove. Any pictures you took are evidence of a crime. I'll write you a receipt for the memory card," he said, moving away to talk to his partner who had been talking to Thom Hark. I sat in the back of the car and waited while the two of them conferred. I noticed Michael Haskins and Dan Berger standing and watching the proceedings. I wondered what Berger's interest was. I was sure that it wasn't just idle curiosity.

~ ~ ~

It was nearly an hour later before Thom and I entered the Smokin' Tuna. Haskins was gone but Dan

Berger was still at the bar. Thom flagged down a waitress to place his order but I walked over and sat down next tor Berger. "You seemed interested in that mess out back. Why would the Feds care about somebody slashing up tourists in Key West?" I asked.

"Who says I give a shit?" Berger turned on his stool to face me.

"Harry Dove, Independent News Service. I was one of the guys that the cops were talking to. I also saw you watching," I introduced myself. I had seen Berger around on the island and up in Miami when I was doing crime stories up there so I knew who he was.

"I know who you are; Dove, but you didn't answer my question."

"You didn't answer mine either. Berger, what is your interest in this case?"

"Go fuck yourself, Dove," Berger said, tossing a twenty on the bar and heading for the door. I ordered a beer and walked over to join Thom Hark who seemed to still be in a bit of shock over the whole ordeal. I dropped into the chair across from him.

"Berger was less than informative," I told him.

"I would imagine so," Thom said, seeming to pull himself out of his foggy state.

"Why is that?" I asked. Sometimes my curiosity gets the better of me.

"Because he's a Fed, Harry. He doesn't need to be informative to a lowly reporter," Thom said, taking a pull on his beer.

"You sure you don't need something stronger than beer, my friend?" I asked.

"I do, but that will have to wait until I get home and don't have to drive anywhere else."

"What did you see in the alley, Thom?" I was curious about what he would say.

"I saw a man brutally murdering a girl," Thom said,

his voice shaking a bit.

"You saw more than that Thom. Describe him."

"A white male, tall and thin, but incredibly strong. It's not easy to cut a throat in one slash, even if the knife is razor sharp. His eyes were awful, filled with rage that he had been caught before he was done with her," Thom swallowed hard.

"That's what I saw too. There was something about that guy that wasn't right," I sighed.

"There's nothing right about a man that would do something like that," Thom shook his head.

"I agree, Thom. Believe me, I agree."

"I think I need to go home," Thom said.

"Is your friend Marlow in town?" I asked. The kid was a damn good investigator.

"No, he's currently working a missing person's case up in Fort Myers," Thom said.

"Too bad, this is something he could sink his teeth into," I sighed. If Marlow was out of town I'd have to handle this one on my own. I had worked with the private investigator on a case a few weeks back that dealt with the death of Ernest Hemingway. The end of the case had been less than satisfying because I couldn't prove anything that I had learned.

"Call me tomorrow, Harry," Thom said, standing and leaving. It was only after he had left that I realized that he had stuck me with the bill. I didn't really mind, because Thom had put me on the lead for a story and I wasn't about to let it go!

~ ~ ~

Sunrise found me awake and waiting at the Police Station for somebody to talk to me about the murder the night before. Neither of the detectives that had been on the scene had shown up for work yet, but that didn't really surprise me. I was hoping to talk to the Chief and I actually caught him as he entered the station.

"Chief Gutierrez, just the man I was hoping to see," I told him. He winced as if I had hit him.

"Mr. Dove. Exactly what have I done to deserve you so early in the morning?" he asked.

I smiled at him. "I wanted to talk to you about the girl that was murdered out behind the Smokin' Tuna last night. I understand that she was the second slashing death in the past week?" I asked.

"Since I just got here and have not seen last night's reports I really can't address that," Gutierrez said.

'That's reasonable, but tell me about the first Slasher killing?"

"No comment, Harry. If there is anything to talk about it will be at the regular press briefing at 10:00 a.m. Now if you will excuse me," Gutierrez stepped into the elevator and the doors slid closed.

I was frustrated, I admit it. Neither the local cops nor the Feds were talking, which mean that there was something up. Something that they didn't want the people to know. Whatever it was, I planned to find out.

~ ~ ~

On Key West, the coconut telegraph is a wonderful thing and it was a good place to pick up tidbits that were not part of the official records. I had headed over to Harpoon Harry's for breakfast. Ron was greeting customers as he usually did. He greeted me and seated me. I slipped him a twenty as I sat down.

"What's that for?" Ron asked.

"What's the telegraph saying about these girls getting cut to pieces?" I asked.

"Not a lot. Just that it is a tall, thin white guy doing the cutting," Ron acknowledged.

"Anything else?" I asked.

"Just that this guy has both the locals and the Feds on edge. Nobody knows why," Ron shrugged.

"Thanks," I told him, waiting for a waitress to come and take my order. I mulled it over as I waited on my food and ate when it arrived. A thought occurred to me. After paying for my meal I picked up my battered Ford station wagon and drove over to the Port Authority to check on what ships had docked in the past week.

With the Feds being involved after the first slasher killing I had a feeling that they had been looking for the killer before he arrived in Key West. The odds were that he had arrived by ship, and I was reasonably certain, that it had been within the past week.

~ ~ ~

Kevin Jenkins had a few minutes free when I arrived. We had a good rapport since I had done a few stories over the years that mentioned what a good job his particular department had done in keeping the ports running smoothly. Jenkins was a short, stout man in his late fifties. His hair had turned white and he had the florid look of a man that either spent too much time in the sun or too much time imbibing in adult beverages. In Jenkins' case I knew it was a little bit of both.

"Harry, what brings you here?" he greeted me, standing up and walking around his desk to shake my hand.

"Can you tell me what ships have docked here in the past week, Kevin?" I asked.

"Sure thing," he said rummaging through some papers on his desk. He gave me a list of ships but I knew it was unlikely I'd be able to get a passenger manifest for any of them. Not from the companies anyway. But when you've been around as long as I have you develop sources for things like that. I shook his hand again and left, heading back to the cop shop for the press briefing, though I was already sure what the Public Information Officer was going to say.

~ ~ ~

The 10:00 a.m. briefing was exactly what I had expected. Yes, two women had been killed, slashed open by an unknown perpetrator. There was no evidence indicating that the two crimes were related and the investigation was on going. I could have written the press release by rote.

I was whistling as I left the briefing because I had something that the cops didn't have and I wasn't ready to share it with them, at least not yet. I had printed out pictures of the Slasher that I had taken the night before and had them in my jacket pocket. The cops had the pictures of the scene and the crowd, but I had pictures of the killer.

The briefing over, I decided to head over to the *Citizen* to check on Thom Hark. I could tell that he was more than a little rattled the night before from what we had seen. At ten years my junior, and lacking my experience in war zones, I knew that he would have a hard time dealing with it all.

~ ~ ~

"Harry, this is certainly a surprise. You swore you'd never darken the *Citizen*'s door again after I fired you back in 1965," Thom Hark noted.

"That was then and this is now, old friend. I take it you had somebody at the briefing?" Harry asked.

"Of course."

"Then you know it was total bullshit."

"I suspect but I don't know that, Harry."

"Berger wouldn't be down here if it wasn't something big. He ranks high enough in the FBI that they wouldn't send him on a whim."

"True enough. So, what do you think is going on?"

"I think this guy is a serial killer and that they have been on his trail for awhile. What I don't understand is why they are working so hard to keep it quiet."

"That certainly is suspect."

"You bet it is. That's why I didn't turn over one of these to the cops," I said tossing a picture of the killer's face onto his desk.

Thom didn't touch it. He looked pained that he was even seeing it again. "I'm trying to forget that face, Harry."

"I understand, Thom, but it is news."

"You love stirring the pot, don't you, Harry?" Thom asked.

"I do," I grinned tipping my straw hat back on my head.

"What do you want me to do with this picture?"

"I want you to run it on tomorrow's front page."

"I can't do that. It will cause a panic."

"What if he kills again tonight?"

"Do you think that will happen?"

"It might. We interrupted him last night, Thom. He wasn't done with whatever he had planned for that girl. So yes, I see him killing again tonight," I told him.

"Damn you, Harry," Thom sighed. I stood and left his office. I had people that I wanted to get that picture out to. They would find him if he was still on the island. And just maybe, I could be there when he struck again!

~ ~ ~

June 11th, 9:45 p.m.

The sun had set and it was getting dark, long dark shadows already settling in streets and alleys across the island. I had a friend working on getting me passenger lists for the ships that had come in before the murders had started but he had warned it might take a day or two. There was nothing I could do about that. All I could do was be out on the streets and mobile in case the Sunset Slasher struck a third time.

I was cruising up and down Duval Street, keeping an eye on the crowds along the sidewalks, the police scanner on the dash giving me a steady dialog of what was going on across the island. Not for the first time I wished that Rick Marlow was around, but he hadn't yet returned from his case up in Fort Myers. I had broken down and called Walter Loomis to ask. Walter was an old adversary but I at least hoped that we had mutual respect for one another.

I was at the south end of Duval Street when I heard the call on the scanner. The suspect had been spotted walking out of Midnight Blues in the company of a young woman. I spun the wheel and stepped on the gas, heading back north along Duval and breaking plenty of traffic laws along the way.

The Slasher didn't even bother dragging her into an alley before he drew his knife and started cutting this time. People were screaming and running in all directions as I ran up on the curb and threw the gearshift into park. I had my camera out and was running forward as several cops arrived. The Slasher continued his grisly work, despite several commands from uniformed cops to freeze. They started shooting and I caught it all on what passes for film in this digital age.

The Slasher was hit multiple times but it never even slowed him down. I got multiple photos of it. Three cops moved in and tried to wrestle him to the ground but he tossed them off as if they were leaves in a hurricane. His knife dipped into the girl's throat one more time and he reached down and tore something loose, then he was off and running.

I ran after him as did several cops, but he managed to lose us. I had again slipped the memory card out of my camera and substituted a blank one. I covered the lens with my hand and snapped off several frames. I hoped that it would be enough to fool the cops.

Once again, I was held for questioning and this

time it was Detective Quintana who arrived to give me the third degree. "Harry Dove. How is it you always turn up when somebody dies?" Quintana asked me.

"Just lucky, I guess. Can you explain to me why that man didn't die? I saw your officers pour several rounds into his body and it didn't seem to faze him," I observed.

"They said you took pictures. Give me the memory card from your camera."

"Those pictures are protected by the first amendment!" I blustered.

"Not this time," Quintana grabbed my camera and ejected the card. I hid my smile as he dropped it into his pocket.

"Do you at least know who that guy was?" I asked.

"Nope," was his succinct response.

"He appeared to tear something out of the body. Can you tell me what it was?" I asked.

"Go home, Harry," Quintana dismissed me and I headed back to my car. I had left the keys in it and was surprised that it hadn't been stolen. Okay, maybe a little insulted too. But I drove straight home and booted up my computer. I wanted to download the pictures and send them to a friend that might be able to help.

I would get the victim's identity in the morning, but for the moment I had enough to write the story and send it to my editor in Miami. He wouldn't be especially happy, but serial killers sold papers. And with the INS being a wire service, they still provided income from papers that were contracted to carry our stories.

~ ~ ~

I added pictures to the five pages of copy that I had written concerning the three deaths and hit *SEND* on the computer. My story would make me no friends on the Key West Police Department but I was okay with that. At least the story would get out.

I walked into my kitchen and pulled a bottle of Scotch from the fridge and poured two fingers over ice. It had been a wild night, and I felt that I was at least entitled to the drink. I planned to make a call on the coroner's office in the morning to find out exactly what the killer had removed from this last body and maybe the other two as well.

~ ~ ~

June 12th, 8:00 a.m.

I was at the coroner's office when she arrived and Gina Clark waved me inside. We were old friends and in exchange for some very expensive bottles of Scotch Gina kept me up to date on the more interesting aspects of her job. This latest victim and the first victim had one other thing in common besides the fact that they were both female. Both had their thyroid gland cut out.

I thought about that for awhile. "Why would the killer take the thyroid gland from his victims?" I asked.

"I have a lot of thoughts, but none of them make sense. The thyroid regulates metabolism," Gina shook her head.

"Would it affect aging?"

"It could. It also regulates muscle development and reflexes."

"That could certainly account for the exhibits of superhuman strength by the killer," I said.

"It could. But how is he distilling what he needs from the thyroid glands of these women?" Gina asked.

"I was hoping you could tell me," Harry told her.

"I wish I could, Harry. But at the moment, I have no clue."

"But you'll call me when you find out?"

"I will," said Gina.

"You are the best, Kid."

"I know," Gina smiled back.

I turned and left the office, leaving just moments before Quintana and Ortiz arrived. I ducked as I drove out of the parking lot, hoping that neither of the two detectives had recognized me. The drive home was short and I fired up my computer. I finally had some leads to pursue.

~ ~ ~

I Googled thyroid excision murders and the screen automatically filled with possibilities. It didn't faze me as I clicked on each individual link and began to read. It didn't take long for me to find a name. I couldn't but help think that the local cops had found it too, but there was still a chance that they had not.

Professor Arkady Declan was a pioneer in thyroid research. His thesis proclaimed that the thyroid could indeed slow the process of aging and give amazing strength to those who could properly distill the hormones from it. Declan had a home in Miami and had until recently been out of the country. Harry sat back and thought about it.

Declan was a specialist on the human thyroid. He had been abroad for more than a year. Harry typed the scientist's name into the search bar.

A picture appeared on the screen and Harry almost jumped in response. It was the same man that he and Thom Hark had seen stabbing the girl behind the Smokin' Tuna. Blinking his eyes to clear away the shock, Harry scrolled through the article.

Arkady Declan specialized in research on hyperthyroidism, which some doctors felt contributed to fits of rage and murder. He had been working for several years to find a cure for it after losing his wife to the disease. I sat back and thought about it for awhile. Then I stood and walked over to the refrigerator and grabbed a Miller Genuine Draft. I unscrewed the top as

I carried it back to the computer, taking it back to the computer and taking a long pull.

I probably should call Chief Gutierrez and give him the name, but I wasn't quite ready to do that. Not without proof. Without proof the cops would just blow me off. No, I needed to sit on it a little longer if I wanted to get the full story. Based on what I had seen the night before, Declan had figured out how to change his appearance.

But there were only a few places on Key West where he could get theatrical grade make-up and wigs. ABC Costumes was one, King's Wigs and Beauty Supplies was the other. It might not be a bad idea to check both places out.

~ ~ ~

June 13th, 9:40p.m.

Cora Sanchez was a tourist. She was visiting Key West for the first, and sadly, the last time. She had lingered on Mallory Square after watching the sunset, waiting for the crowds to fade. A man caught her interest. He was alone, sitting on a bench and staring off into the darkness at the invisible ocean beyond the end of the Square. He was tall and thin and pale, with straight dark hair. His eyes seemed to be exceptionally blue in the lamplight.

"Hi there," Cora said. "Do you mind if I sit with you for a bit?" The man looked startled, glancing around the area as if to make sure this wasn't some sort of joke. They were the only two people around, at least within shouting distance.

"Not at all. Please, have a seat," he replied, scooting over to allow her room. He looked down at his feet, as if he were very shy.

"I'm Cora. I'm here on vacation," she told him, smiling.

"This is a good place to get away to," he nodded.

"Have you been here before?"

"Not for a long time. I used to bring my wife here before ..." his words died away.

"Oh, I didn't realize you were married," Cora said apologetically.

"I'm not anymore. She died some years back. But we used to watch the sunset and then sit here afterwards talking into the wee hours of the night," he said.

"I'm sorry for your loss. Were you together long?"

"Ten years."

"That's a long time."

"We were supposed to have a lifetime. But it didn't work out that way. She suffered from a medical condition."

"Cancer?"

"Hyperthyroidism."

"I've heard of it. It is a pretty bad disease?" she asked.

"It is. It drove her crazy."

"I'm so sorry ... I guess I don't know your name."

"My name is Arkady."

"I'm so sorry, Arkady. Is there anything I can do for you?"

"Just sit here with me and look out at the sea like Miranda used to do. That would help me a lot," Arkady told her.

"I can do that," Cora told him, smiling. She looked out at the sea. She never saw the blade that sliced her throat open, or felt the man cutting out her thyroid gland afterwards. All Cora Sanchez knew was that her life ended.

I got there right behind the police. This was the third victim from which he had removed the thyroid. I wondered how many how many he needed for whatever his purpose was. I took several photos and this time the cops didn't bother to take them.

I left before the detectives got there. I had a feeling that I knew where Declan might be. I made my way to a small motel that stood just between Key West and Stock Island. I had a feeling. I opened the door and walked inside.

The kid in the office was thin and had a bad case of acne. He had wide brown eyes and short brown hair. His name was Harvey. "I'm looking for someone," I told him.

"I don't know anybody," he raised his hands.

"I doubt that."

"Too bad."

"I have a fifty that says different," I said.

"For fifty, I might."

"I figured."

"I'm looking for a tall, thin guy, dark hair. Might have signed in under Arkady or Declan," I told him.

"I remember him. He's a pretty spooky guy."

"What is his room number?"

"Room 238."

"Thanks, I said, heading for the stairs. I had a bad feeling about Arkady Declan. I knew I was too late to help his latest victim, but I was sure I could help capture him. I made my way to the door and knocked.

To my surprise, nobody answered. Could it be he wasn't back yet? Or had he found another place to do whatever it was that he was doing with the dead women's thyroid glands? I figured if I went back and slipped Harvey another fifty he might be talked into letting me have a spare key for Declan's room. This story was getting expensive between the Scotch for the Medical Examiner and bribing desk clerks. Still, the story would be worth it. If I lived to write it.

Harvey didn't look particularly happy to see me reappear in front of his desk. So, I let him get a look at the second fifty before I said a word. "What now?" he asked sounding really put upon.

"I need a look in Mr. Creepy's room," I waved the fifty just out of his reach.

"You're gonna get me fired, Dude."

"Not if nobody finds out."

"Shit. I can use the cash," Harvey sighed, slipping the extra room key across the desk. I handed him the fifty, picked up the key and headed back out the door. The night was pulling in close, making it darker and the shadows had a way of seeming more sinister as the night closed in. I couldn't help but feel a chill race down my spine.

Despite the chill, I was sweating as I approached the room for the second time. What the hell was I doing? I wasn't a cop; I was a reporter. And yet, here I was, making myself part of the story by doing things that a cop should be doing. Except I wasn't sure that the cops were even looking in this guy's direction. I paused to take a deep breath and let it out slowly, trying to calm my racing heart.

I knocked once again with the same results, no sound of movement from inside or answer. I slipped the key into the lock and turned it. The door opened under my hand. I pushed the door open and stepped inside. It took only an instant to find the light switch. I flipped it on and the room was suddenly alight.

It looked like any other cheap motel room with pasteboard furniture. The carpet was threadbare and the beds were undisturbed. Clearly Declan hadn't been here since the maid had cleaned the room this morning. I had to wonder if he was even going to come back at all.

I looked through everything but there was nothing there to find. I walked out and headed back to the office to return the key. I was almost there when a car pulled into the parking lot. The headlights missed me, but I managed to get a look at the man behind the wheel. It was Arkady Declan.

I kept walking away from his room as he swung the car into the parking space and climbed out. He carried a small plastic bag in one hand as he headed up the steps to his second-floor room. I made up my mind and pulled out my cell phone and dialed 911. The dispatcher picked up. "911 – What is your emergency?" she asked.

"I'm at the ..." I gave the name of the motel. "The man that's been cutting up women just pulled in here and is going into one of the rooms," I told her.

"I'll send cars right away. Can you please stay on the line?" she asked.

I could have, but I didn't. I broke the connection, keeping my eyes on the room. I wanted to see the cops nail this guy for a multitude of reasons, not the least of which I wanted to see if they would have any better luck than the cops that had tried to get him the night before.

It didn't take long for them to arrive and I was watching when they did. The results were what I had expected. Arkady Declan raced out of the room, causing several injuries along the way before climbing into his car and driving off. I thought about waiting for Quintana and Ortiz and decided against it.

I would talk to the Chief in the morning and lay my theory out for him. If he would accept it or not, I had no idea. But at least he would hear it.

~ ~ ~

June 14th 8:00 a.m.

I was waiting at the police station when Chief Gutierrez arrived. He looked even less happy to see me than usual, which was saying something and it was nothing good. "What do you want?" he asked in a tone that indicated he had tasted something bad.

"I want to talk to you about the Sunset Slasher," I

said.

"Nice of you to share those pictures with us, Dove. We might have caught the bastard by now if we had them *before* they were printed in the newspaper," the Chief replied angrily.

"I was just doing my job, Chief."

"What I should do is toss your ass in jail for impeding a police investigation. Now I repeat, what the hell do you want?"

"I think your killer is a former doctor named Arkady Declan. He used to specialize in the field of Hyperthyroidism. He lost his wife to the disease and according to what I've been able to find out, he's cutting the thyroids out of his victims and taking them with him. Would you care to comment?" I figured to at least give him a chance.

"Go fuck yourself, Dove. And get out of my office!" Knowing I would get nothing else, I left, stepping out into the hot morning sun. The humidity was already climbing so I stripped off my coat and headed for my car. I was hungry and Harpoon Harry's wasn't far away. I was curious if Ron had picked up any word on the killings from the coconut telegraph. I got into my car and drove over.

Harpoon Harry's was busy as usual for this time of day. I had a feeling that people felt a little easier moving around in daylight than they were beginning to feel about being out after dark. Ron was out front greeting customers like he normally did when I walked in. He took one look at me and acted like he had just bitten into a rotten apple and found a worm. I walked over to find out why.

"What have I done to you that you greet me like that?" I asked.

"How about that Sunset Slasher shit you been putting in the papers? Business is off from it," Ron hissed.

"Place looks packed to me," I said making a point to look around.

"Sure, during the day. But folks are staying away in droves at night. Sales are way down from about 7 o'clock on."

"The cops will get him soon, Ron. Then the tourists will come back."

"You better hope so, Harry," he said and I walked to the back and found a small table to myself. The only person that approached my table was a waitress to take my order. Bacon and eggs with fried potatoes and a Café Con Leche. I was halfway through it when a shadow fell over my table. It was the Fed, Dan Berger.

Berger was a portly sort of man with craggy good looks and thick brown hair and brown eyes. He exuded an aura that said don't fuck with me and the expression on his face was not one that expressed any sort of brotherly love. "I want to talk to you, Dove."

"So, have a seat, it's a free country. But I'd suggest ordering something, Ron is a bit touchy today," I told him.

"He ain't the only one. I just got done talking to Chief Gutierrez. You've been obstructing justice, Ass hat. By withholding those pictures, you have allowed a wanted felon to continue preying on the people of Key West. If I wanted to, and believe me I'm this fucking close," he held up his hand and held thumb and forefinger less than a quarter of an inch apart, "to hauling your ass in and putting you in a fucking federal prison as a material witness! So, if you want to save your sorry broken down ass, Dove, you better start talking to me and you better play it damn straight!"

"Sure thing. What do you want to know?" I asked. At this point playing it completely straight with the feds seemed to be the best idea.

"Tell me about this Arkady Declan guy you're so hot for," Berger commanded. So, I did. I gave Berger everything, even stuff that the Chief of Police hadn't wanted to hear. After I was done talking, we both sat there in silence and I finished cleaning my plate. The waitress came and got it and left me a second Café Con Leche as well as one for Berger.

Customers came and went around us as Berger digested what I had told him. It was a lot to take in and even I had to admit that a good bit of it was nothing more than pure speculation. But somehow Berger seemed to buy it. "Okay, Dove, it's weird, but it makes sense. You think this guy is some kind of nutcase that is stealing women's thyroids because he thinks they give him longer life, faster reflexes, and superhuman strength."

"I think he believes that, yes. I didn't say I believe it," I told him.

"Semantics, Dove. You said that you saw this guy take multiple hits from gunfire by cops last night and yet he seemed to shrug it off like it was nothing."

"That's what I saw. The statements from the cops should verify it," I pointed out.

"They do. So, what do you think this nutcase is going to do next?"

"I wish I knew," I told him.

"Gimme your cell phone number. I want to be able to reach you if anything pops on this guy," he said. I wrote it on a napkin and handed it to him. Then Dan Berger left, leaving me, I noticed, with the tab not only for my meal but his drink as well. A small price to pay to keep the feds off my back.

~ ~ ~

I spent the day doing more background research on Arkady Declan. From articles I could pull up on line I had discovered that similar murders had occurred in

66

Miami not long after his wife had succumbed to her illness. Declan had then left for Europe, allegedly to confer with specialists in hyperthyroidism abroad. In every country that he went to, every major city, there had been a rash of slasher style murders. In every case, the victims' thyroid gland had been excised.

By this point, I know what you're thinking. You're thinking that perhaps I have succumbed to my own personal form of insanity. All I am doing is reporting the facts of the case as I learned them. Am I delusional? I don't think so, but delusional people rarely do. So, I leave it for you, dear reader, to follow the facts and make that critical determination on your own.

~ ~ ~

Sunset, Mallory Square.

By nightfall I was on the square, watching the magnificent Key West sunset with hundreds of other people. But I was scanning the crowd, looking for the face that I had become well acquainted with over the past few days. I had no doubt that I would find him this night, hunting his prey like any predator in the wild.

I had no idea what I might do if I caught him, but I knew that I would do whatever I could to stop him from killing again. I don't know why, perhaps because of superstitions in my family background, but I had a small .380 loaded up with silver bullets that I had a local gunsmith make. Silver was supposed to work on both vampires and werewolves, so why not on some thyroid-stealing ghoul?

I worked my way through the crowd, both a small tape recorder and a digital camera in my pockets just in case I needed to document events this night. I had a feeling that Declan would strike again. Whatever he needed the thyroids for, three would not be enough. I watched as the sun slipped below the horizon, no green flash evident on this particular night. The green flash is supposed to mean good luck for anyone who might see it.

This apparently was not my lucky night. I took a seat on an empty bench and watched as the crowd thinned, most of them moving towards Duval Street and the never-ending action there.

I frowned. How could I have been so wrong? But then I noticed I wasn't the only person sitting alone on a bench.

I got up and started walking toward the man sitting on the other bench. He seemed young, with longer dark hair and pale skin. He fit the build of the killer and matched the looks based on both pictures and description. I would know more once I got close enough to see his face.

The sky was growing dark as I approached. I resisted the urge to touch the .380 holstered on my hip. That would be a dead giveaway. He looked up as I approached, his eyes piercing. They gave me pause.

"Can I help you?" he asked, his voice as sibilant as the hissing of a snake, his eyes had an almost hypnotic quality.

"Are you Arkady Declan?" I asked, finding some inner reservoir of courage that I didn't know I possessed.

"Do I know you?" he asked.

"My name is Harry Dove," I told him. He stood and I pulled out my pistol. Arkady Declan ran for the edge of the pier and I put five shots into his back. He tumbled over into the water and disappeared.

Suddenly Mallory Square was alive with police vehicles. Boats were called out and the area was dragged for a body. None was ever found. I was put in cuffs and taken to the Key West Police Station and given an audience with the Chief himself. He and Dan Berger told me that if I ever breathed a word or tried to file the story, I would be arrested for murder as they had surveillance tapes that showing I had quite deliberately shot a stranger five times in the back. I had no choice but to give in to their wishes and not file what could well have been the story of the new century.

So instead I put it before you as a work of fiction. Only those who were involved will recognize the truth, thinly disguised as a rambling fantasy of an old drunken reporter.

The authorities will call this story pure fiction, a whim created for its sensationalistic aspects. But there were no more slasher murders on Key West. The local police and the Feds closed the cases, saying they had been the work of a transient. But I know better. And now so do you. I kept my mouth shut, and I am still alive and working. I can't say that the same would have been true if I had pursued the true story of the Sunset Slasher until its end ...

Sometimes Murder, Isn't Murder

Justin Maxwell

Captain Bama was known by Key West charter captains as a smart fisherman, a good captain and sometimes one mean son-of-a-bitch. At 43 years old, he had lived in Key West for 25 years. Since moving there from Mobile in the 1980's, he had worked as a bartender, a smuggler, a short order cook, a first mate and now he was the captain of his own fishing boat; *Reel Anger*. Over the years he lived with a few women and married a couple too.

Brenda was new and different. She was a widow who moved to Key West to escape the boredom of her previous life. She said Cleveland just didn't do it for her anymore. She had been the good wife, helping her husband build their successful insurance agency from the ground up, stood by his side when he ran for city council in an ill-fated attempt to begin a political career, and held his hand as he lay dying from a massive heart attack. Brenda sold the business and moved to the land of sunshine, buying a condominium on the south side of the island overlooking the Atlantic and quickly embraced the party atmosphere that is at the heart of Key West.

One day as she was having a drink at Schooner Wharf, she was attracted to a man at the bar. He was dressed in a well-worn straw cowboy hat, a white tee shirt advertising Reel Anger Charter Service, and what first caught Brenda's attention, tight jeans. No longer the mild, meek dutiful wife of a businessman and potential future governor of Ohio, Brenda walked to the bar, sat next to the man she was admiring and asked the bartender for a refill. As she waited she smiled listening to the man's Alabama accent. As the bartender placed the drink on the bar, Bama said, "Put it on my bill, will ya, Toby."

That was how Brenda and Bama met. He was a rugged man of the sea and she a sophisticated woman. They dated, Bama moved into her condo and they rented out his house. She adored his southern drawl, lack of refinement, and sexual appetite, and she was so much different than the women he had been with; she carried herself with dignity and class, she was beautiful and below that cultured exterior she was a generous and adventurous lover. Marriage seemed the be the natural next step, but in the years since they met Bama found that Brenda's desires went beyond the simplicity of a monogamous marriage, she enjoyed the company of other men, a problem that was the cause of much of their marital strife.

Three years later, Bama stopped at the post office to pick up a package that arrived in Brenda's name. He threw it in the back seat of his truck and drove to Kmart where he selected a bright yellow helium-filled balloon with a smiley face on one side and the words "Happy

Birthday" on the reverse. He also bought a roll of blue crepe paper, the kind used for party streamers. In the parking lot, Bama used his knife to open the package and took the Remington semi-automatic shotgun out of the cellophane packing sleeve. Bama loaded the gun and placed it in his duffle bag. He opened the glove compartment and removed a Glock 40-caliber semi-auto pistol. Bama wrapped it in a towel and placed it in the duffle and zipped the bag closed.

As the engines warmed, Bama tossed the bag in his boat and talked to his buddy who went by the nickname, Billy Buoy. "Don't let the wind blow yer hat off," Billy Buoy said. Bama took the old straw cowboy hat off and tossed it to his old friend saying, "Here, you keep it for me." He cast the lines off and slowly motored through the harbor to open water. He passed Mallory Square where the street entertainers performed for tips each evening at the Sunset Celebration. When he first arrived in Key West, he dressed up as a clown and tied balloons into animals.

Bama set the GPS, sat back, opened a can of beer and enjoyed the warmth of the sun on his weathered face. After 36 minutes, he slowed the boat and tossed his third beer can over the side and gathered the items he needed; a black twenty-foot, 5/8's inch dock line, the shotgun and pistol, the crepe paper and the smiley face balloon. Then he removed the shoelace from his left shoe. He tied the lace tightly around the steering wheel in a loop and slid his hand through it testing to make sure it would easily fit in later on. Bama cut two pieces of the crepe paper 18 inches long and braided them into a short length of paper rope. He tied the string from the balloon to one end of the crepe paper rope and the other end was tied to the trigger guard of the pistol. He placed the shotgun across his legs and pulled the dock line around his waist, tying it tightly. He sucked in his stomach and pulled at the rope until the knot was behind him. Bama pushed the throttle forward and the boat gained speed as he took the shotgun, aimed and shot a whole in the bottom of the boat. Bama was pleased with his choice of shotgun shell. The buckshot made a large hole in the bottom and water began rushing in. Bama threw the shotgun over the side and lowered the throttle full. The boat was taking on water but increasing in speed and managed to cover the remaining three miles when the GPS beeped indicating he had arrived at his destination.

Bama stopped and seawater sloshed inside the boat. He slid his left hand in the shoelace tied to the wheel gripping the loose end of the lace with his teeth and pulled it tight. Once he was sure the boat would sink he took the Glock with the attached yellow helium-filled balloon, raised the gun to his head as far back as his torn rotator cuff would allow and pulled the trigger.

Bama's body slumped forward, the dock line tied around his waist secured him to the helm, the pistol fell from his hand, the .40-caliber bullet entered the lower back of his skull and exited through his forehead.

As the boat slipped below the waves, the balloon floated free and rose to the surface. It would be pushed along by the wind for miles until the crepe paper rope denigrated and the pistol dropped to the bottom and the balloon floated off on the breeze.

~ ~ ~

"Ladies and gentlemen welcome aboard *The Mermaid*. I'm Captain Grant and I'll be at the helm for today's voyage out on the waters of the Atlantic Ocean. Gather around the railing and look down through the glass bottom of the boat. Through that glass today you will see ancient coral, giant sea rays, sea turtles, shipwrecks and maybe a man-eating shark or two." It was the same tour twice a day.

The course *The Mermaid* would follow took the boat through Key West Bight, past Mallory Square and out into open water. Captain Grant would first take the tourists to a pile of ballast stones that are all that remains of a Spanish galleon that sunk centuries ago.

Captain Grant announced; "The shipwreck was part of a Spanish treasure fleet that was carrying millions of dollars in gold, silver, and gems." The guests lined the railing with their cameras and cell phones snapping photographs of the pile of stones and the fish that called it home; triggerfish swam nearby, a lobster scurried back into the protection of its liar, sergeant-majors and an eel swam around seemingly unaware of the boat.

As *The Mermaid* slowly drifted over the remains of the galleon the captain hyped the experience by asking for a moment of silence out of respect for the crew of the ship who lost their lives when the ship was broken apart in a ferocious hurricane. Of course, not knowing anything about the ship, he had no idea if anyone was killed when the ship grounded.

As the captain stood at the wheel, the respectful silence of the passengers suddenly turned to screams of fear. As *The Mermaid* slowly drifted over the sandy bottom, a 28-foot center-council powerboat lying upright on the bottom came into view. Sitting at the helm of the boat was a man, his eyes stared off in the distance, his graying hair flowed in the current, his face was pale white and small fish nibbled at the large opening blown in the man's head.

Deputy Radak of the Monroe County Sheriff's Department was assigned to investigate the homicide of Captain Christopher "Bama" Hughey. During his investigation, the deputy learned the grieving widow was known to have had many male "friends" and was rumored to be having an affair with the manager of the drugstore who rented Bama's house. He checked her phone records and found 28 calls made between the widow and the renter in the last three weeks. He also discovered that Brenda's credit card was used to purchase a shotgun just days before a similar weapon was used to blow a hole in the bottom of *Reel Anger*. The renter of Bama's house and suspected lover of Bama's wife, Craig Willard, held a concealed weapon license and a search of the rental house turned up a Glock semi-automatic .40 caliber pistol, the same caliber that killed Bama. The authorities determined the weapon had been recently fired and Mr. Willard tested positive for gunshot residue.

The evidence against Bama's wife and her lover was overwhelming. They were arrested for the murder of Captain Christopher "Bama" Hughey. Their lawyers argued that the two were not romantically involved and the phone calls were about an infestation of palmetto bugs in the rental house, and Mr. Willard claimed he had been shooting his Glock in the mangroves on Big

Pine Key days before the murder. At one point during the trial the prosecuting attorney asked the defendants, "What are you going to say next, that Captain Bama tied himself to the boat and shot himself?" eliciting a laugh from those in the court.

The abundance of evidence was overwhelming and both defendants were found guilty and sentenced to life in prison.

After the trial, Billy Buoy along with several other charter captains, sat at a bar toasting Bama and telling stories of their fellow captain and friend. Billy pushed the old well-worn straw cowboy hat higher up on his head, took a long swig of his beer and said, "Bama told me he figured out a way to make sure it was the last time that bitch was gonna cheat on him."

Malloy's Ex

Barthélemy Banks

Malloy's elbows were on the bar at Margaritaville – the Jimmy Buffett café on Duval Street, not the resort on the waterfront near Mallory Square. On the small stage Caffeine Carl and the Buzz were playing, not Jimmy Buffet. Malloy was thinking of ordering a Cheeseburger in Paradise, one of the best burgers on the island. It went well with a frozen margarita. He'd had three.

Someone sat down on the stool beside him. Malloy had good peripheral vision. It was a big man with a familiar slouch.

"Hello, G," he said. That was the CIA cryptonym for George Magaddino.

"Need to talk with you, M."

Malloy – M to members of Operation 40, the CIA's assassination squad – drained his margarita, then turned to look at the man sitting next to him at the beer-stained bar. Black wavy hair, dark circles under the eyes, obviously a man of Italian heritage. He was wearing a $1,194 Gieves & Hawkes sharkskin suit, which made him stand out like the proverbial feces in the punchbowl. A field agent, but not very good at tradecraft. He should know better than call attention to himself like this.

"What's up?" Tim Malloy had not worked for the

CIA for several years. They had no use for drunks whose gun hand had begun to shake. He thought of himself as retired, but that was just another word for unemployed. He drew a government pension, not a lot, but enough that he could spend his afternoons here at Margaritaville in Key West.

"Somebody has Kathy."

Kathy was Malloy's ex-wife. And George Magaddino's current wife.

"Has? As in kidnapped?"

"She always said you were smart. Didn't see it till now."

Malloy studied the man, trying to decide whether to coldcock him or not. He sighed. No point in it. They would wind up in jail if they got into a bar fight. KWPD was pretty strict about that.

"Why are you telling me this?" said Malloy, the moment of contemplating violence having passed.

"I need your help to get her back."

Malloy signaled for another margarita. "Why would I want to do that? She dumped me. Ran off with my old partner before taking up with you."

"Because I'm on my own. This isn't a Company operation. She's being held here in Key West and I don't have anyone else to turn to."

Malloy looked up. "You love her, don't you?"

"Of course."

No need to hate this doofus. Kathy had left him for J, not G. George came later. "Why isn't Langley involved?" he asked out of curiosity.

"I'm no longer with the Company. We parted ways last June."

Malloy said, "Your decision or theirs?"

"Theirs. Got caught with my hand in the cookie jar."

"Yeah, Kathy has expensive tastes."

"Will you help me?" G looked anxious, on the verge of panic. Must be true that someone was holding his wife.

"Look, I've been out of it longer than you. I don't even have a gun."

"That's a sad statement for a former shooter. But don't worry, I've got an extra weapon, a Mac-10."

"Jeez, where'd you get one of them? From Mitch WerBell?" Dead for nearly thirty-five years, Mitchell Livingston WerBell III was the mercenary who developed the revolutionary sound suppressor for the Mac-10.

"No," replied G, not getting the joke. "Got a pair of them from a drug dealer in Miami. They were expensive, but the Company never recovered all the money I appropriated.

The Military Armament Company model 10 – Mac-10, for short – was a compact, blowback operated machine pistol. It had been outlawed by the 1994 Assault Weapons Ban, mainly because it had a threaded barrel to accommodate a suppressor, and its magazine would hold 32 rounds. Mac-10s became the weapon of choice for South Florida drug dealers until the TEC-9 came along.

"Do you know where Kathy's being held?"

G nodded. "Yes, room 407 in La Concha. I'm supposed to meet them there in twenty minutes and give them $2.7 million in exchange for Kathy."

"$2.7 million? That's a lot of money. Where would

you get that?"

"That's how much I found in that cookie jar. But I've only got about $1 million left, so I couldn't meet their terms if I wanted to."

Malloy finished off his frozen margarita too fast. It gave him a brain freeze. "I take it that cookie jar didn't belong to the company."

"Well, it did, but I was supposed to give it to these guys to start a small revolution in South America. I didn't."

"What's your plan?" He held his tongue against the roof of his mouth, the prescribed "cure" for a brain freeze.

"Kill them, of course."

"Why did you buy two Mac-10s?"

"Because I knew I could find you sitting here at the bar in Margaritaville."

"You were that sure I'd help?"

"No. But I got a good price on buying two guns."

"If I help you, do I get half of the money that's left?"

"Nope."

"If we kill them, do you get Kathy?"

"Yep."

"Well, I guess that's a good deal. I don't want her back."

The two men stood. Malloy threw two twenties on the bar and G picked up his duffle bag. They walked a block down Duval Street to La Concha Hotel. Malloy showed him how to enter through Starbucks and take a hallway to an elevator. They were halfway to the fourth floor when G opened the duffle and extracted two semiautomatic machine pistols.

Malloy checked his, inspected the magazine. The 32 9mm cartridges grinned up at him like copper teeth. He slammed the metal magazine back into the gun and pulled back on the receiver to cock it. "How do you want to go about this?" he asked.

"Kick in the door."

"Risky. We don't know how solid the door is. You could break a foot without accomplishing anything more than letting them know you're outside."

"You got a better idea?"

Malloy nodded. "Knock on the door. When they open it, go in shooting."

"We might hit Kathy."

"Not likely," said Mallow as the elevator stopped at the fourth floor. "They'll probably have her in the bedroom or bathroom. The 9s probably won't go through the wall."

"You sure you're sober enough to do this?"

"Does the pope roller-skate?"

"Well –"

"Hey, you came to me. I didn't ask for this nifty Mac-10."

"Okay, okay. I'm just nervous. I'm not a professional shooter like you."

"Like I used to be. Haven't killed anybody in days."

As they approached room 402, Malloy held up a finger to signal that G keep quiet. "Don't hesitate," he whispered. "Go in shooting."

Knock, knock.

"Yo, that you Georgie Porgie?" said a voice on the other side of the door.

Malloy nodded an okay and G answered, "It's me."

83

As the door started to open, Malloy kicked it, sending the man on the other side reeling backward. Mallory was first in, shooting as he entered. There were four of them. He took out three; G got the last one.

Malloy stared down at the dead men. "These aren't Hispanics," he noted.

"Didn't say they were." G stepped around one of the victims to open the bedroom door.

"Hold it," warned Malloy, but he was too late.

Ka-bam. The bullet caught G in the throat and he went down like dropping a bag of Gold Metal flour.

Tat-tat-tat. Malloy shot the man who had been babysitting Kathy.

"Damn," he said as he checked G. Dead as an armadillo on a Florida interstate. He walked over to his ex-wife and worked the duct tape free from her wrists, ankles, and mouth. Her lipstick came off with the tape.

"Is George dead?"

"Get used to being a widow." He bent down to check the pockets of the last man he'd shot. There he found the federal ID he'd expected. These had been Company men. They had been holding George's wife to lure him in. After stealing their money he'd been on the run.

"Now what?" said Kathy, looking down at her dead husband.

"You'd better get out of here quick. Even with the suppressors, people heard these shots. Police will be on the way."

"Take me with you."

Malloy snorted. "I don't want you."

"I'll be your wife again. I know you'd like that."

"No way."

"I know where the $1 million dollars is hidden."

"Welcome back," said Malloy.

The Missing Max

Jack Mazur

Joe Beans and I were a bit worried that our other old good friend hadn't shown up. We knew he was in town because we'd had drinks with him three nights previous down at the Green Parrot. Was supposed to meet us the next day for a fishing excursion on my boat.

It wasn't all that odd for Max to miss an appointment. He had been employed by the CIA and other dark clouds for years. Joe and I had met him in the Ia Drang Valley, Republic of Vietnam, back in '68. He was working for Air America. He was a good guy, liked his beer and would sometimes light up a joint right outside of the Officer's Club at Cam Ran Bay. Max was an officer, or, appeared to be. Joe Beans and I would steal officer's insignia and gain entrance. Insignia was easy to get as no one would wear it in the field. Officers were the first to get shot. We'd all get blasted then go our separate ways. But we always made plans to meet again and no one ever skipped out on each other. This not showing up stuff was a bit out of character.

So Joe and I hit the streets asking all the bartenders we knew if they had seen Max. Of course we had a few beers along the way. He hadn't been around. Out on the sidewalk we quickly found that we were being tailed. It wasn't rocket science. None of the bars we hit were in any kind of sensible order. Besides, a transgender in a sundress with two days growth on his face ain't hard to spot. Two days growth and bulging biceps! Gotta love this town! Our plan was quick and in the Three Stooges School of Comedy. I crossed the street and doubled back around while Joe Beans suddenly turned to confront the guy or the fake girl or whatever. While Joe pretended to have verbal hallucinations I got behind the guy and then got on all fours. Joe simply pushed him over me. Kind of fun actually. I do have to say the guy had on a pair of really nice undies from Victoria's Secret. Same ones I'd bought for my girlfriend. Black! I preferred red.

Being followed isn't fun so Joe and I roughed him up a bit without leaving any marks. Being mid-day in the middle of May didn't hurt as there was no traffic and no witnesses.

"Alright, motherfuck, why you following us", said Joe. The guy, in a deep baritone, said he wasn't following anybody. Joe kicked him in the groin. I don't think the black panties served as any protection. "Hey, Jack, what you wanna do with this guy?" I wanted to kick him again so I did. Didn't know I had the propensity for such violence. We dragged him under a Poinsettia tree then I went to the Bottlecap and got three cold beers. When I returned our queen had a few more injuries. Too bad. I gave him a beer, which he cried into. He did start talking though. And it had everything to do with Max.

Somewhere along the line Max had met another old associate from Air America. They'd had dinner downtown but the dinner was witnessed by several of his friend's cohorts. The old friend from Air America had turned a really rough corner in his life. And he had heard a rumor from a sheriff's deputy that Max and the County Sheriff had killed a member of his "posse." No truer words were ever spoken. The sheriff and Max had killed a serial child molester under a bridge in the upper keys. Threw the body to the bull sharks who just happened to be hanging around. The queen said the old friend and some others had kidnapped Max in his sleep and they were holding him somewhere in the Saddlebunch Keys. In an old camp way out in the mangroves.

That wasn't too tough to figure out. It was Dieter's old campground. Dieter, the former U-boat captain who had his submarine shot out from under him in 1943 and who had lived in the swamps for 50 years before his death. I had buried him. I had burned down his camp and later rebuilt it. Joe, Max, and I spent a lot of time there. Drank a lot of beer, did a lot of fishing and sometimes one or the other of us would camp out there for a week by ourselves just to get our shit together. It was an unfindable location. We thought.

"Okay, Freddie Mercury," I said. "Get Max to the Bottlecap Bar in three hours and there won't be anymore bullsharks." He got up, straightened his skirt, and was off. Joe Beans was a little antsy but he kept it together. I bought him two shots of tequila. I did not indulge.

Three hours later, to the minute, Max was in the Bottlecap looking no worse for the wear. It was great to see him and all three of us relaxed. THEN I had a tequila! We told Max what we had done and how we had saved his miserable ass. He looked at us strangely. Nobody had shown up in a sundress with a three-day-old beard and said anything. He'd taken care of himself with his old buddy. The first thing he said was that his old ex-buddy wouldn't be marrying anyone soon of any gender.

He pulled out a pack of smokes from his shirt pocket. He tapped on the packet and out fell a human ring finger! Complete with wedding band. We sashayed down to the Green Parrot for a night of whatever came by. Two days later he was working for some other dark cloud and doing whatever it is he does. Joe and I dug

The Missing Max

up some officer insignias and bullshitted our way onto Boca Chica and the Officer's Club.

How Did

You Die?

Robert Coburn

They spoke in whispers though there wasn't a living
soul around other than themselves.
Rebecca giggled.
"Shhh..." Bill Archer cautioned her. "Somebody'll

call the cops."

Charley Wright stifled a laugh.

"You said *body*," he croaked hoarsely behind his hand. "We're surrounded by them."

Irene Evans made a snuffling sound through her nose.

"That's so funny," she finally got out.

"C'mon, guys," Bill said, laughing now himself. "You want to get us busted?"

"Pass me that joint," Charley asked Irene.

The four friends sat on the ground in a grassy space hidden behind two mausoleums. Night had long settled in the cemetery, the gates having been locked hours earlier.

"Any wine left?" Rebecca slurred.

Rebecca Sloan had come down to Key West from Ohio on vacation two years ago and stayed. Common story. She and Irene are roommates. Both worked on a sunset cruise boat.

"This has got to be the best weed in the world," Charley pronounced. "Where'd you get it, Bill?"

Charley Wright has lived on the island three years. Dropped out of college after his second year. He crews on one of the parachute boats. He'd turned Irene and Rebecca onto the cruise boat gig. They took care of each other that way.

"Got a buddy lives in Denver," Bill told him. "Crazy mother. Mailed me the shit, if you can believe that. Thought the post office had sniffer dogs for this stuff. They must've had a cold."

Bill Archer was the oldest of the group but not by much. He tends bar at the Straw Hat, a small watering hole off the Key West Bight.

"Let's play the game," Irene said. "I think it's Rebecca's turn."

"Wake up, Rebecca," Charley said, nudging her gently. "Game time. You're on."

~~~

Officer Louis Crandal cruised slowly on Olivia Street past the 19-acre cemetery set in the center of town, his eyes scanning the grounds. There'd been reports of disturbances there. He noticed nothing unusual. The street lamps seemed to make the night even blacker beyond where the light fell off. He turned left on Frances and drove down it to Angela where he took another left and started drifting down it. Approaching Grinnel Street, he got a call about a fight outside a bar on upper Duval. He hit the rack- lights and sped away.

~~~

The game went like this. They had to tell how they came to be in the cemetery. That is, how they'd died. No one knew whose idea it'd been. Just sprang up one night.

There'd been five of them at the beginning. They were regulars at the bar where Bill worked. One night someone had mentioned an old Lenny Bruce record album cover he'd seen for sale on eBay—a photo of the comedian enjoying a slice of watermelon at a picnic over a grave. Not one of them had a clue who Lenny Bruce might have been but they loved the idea of having a picnic at the graveyard. Wouldn't that be a hoot, Devany had said—that was Walter Devany, an electrician's helper. He was no longer part of the group, much to everyone's relief. But on that particular night, Walt had suggested they go out to the cemetery and smoke some dope. So when the bar closed, Bill grabbed a couple bottles of wine and they all snuck into the cemetery. It'd been a moonless night but the tombstones and crypts had still shown white against the blackness, adding to the creepiness. They'd found a concealed spot to climb over the fence and then made their way to the center of the grounds. It all was deliciously scary and everyone had gotten stoned out of their minds. Walt had been right. It was a hoot. It became a monthly thing, usually on a new moon but not always.

~~~

"So how'd it happen, Rebecca?" Bill asked. "What brought you to this charming place?"

Rebecca giggled.

"Could I have some more wine first?"

Charley lit another joint and passed it to her. Irene topped up her plastic cup. Rebecca took a long drink followed by a couple of hits.

""Well, I think I died in my sleep," she said, breathing out. "I don't remember exactly."

She giggled again. They all did.

"You said that the last time, Rebecca," Bill laughed. "What a boring way to go. Charley here drowned. Fell out of the parachute or something. Irene, what the hell happened to you, Irene? Oh, yeah, you were the vampire woman. Got a stake in the heart. See how much better that is, Rebecca? Even our former friend, weirdo Walt, had a good one. Electrocuted. And me, got shot trying to stop a holdup. Very heroic death. You,

Rebecca? Died in your sleep. Hardly worth the effort."

They all laughed. Irene refilled Rebecca's cup. Someone passed around another joint.

"Hey, did you see that?' Charley whispered excitedly. "Police car on Angela."

"Told you jerks to be quiet," Bill said angrily. "Maybe we oughta split."

They scrambled to get to their feet.

"Oh, man, I'm stiff," Charley complained. "Somebody wake up Rebecca."

"She's out cold," Bill said, shaking the girl. "Let's go."

"We can't just leave her," Irene said.

"What are we going to do?" Bill snapped. "Carry her? How the hell are we going to get her over the fence? Let her sleep it off here. Nothing's going to happen."

"I suppose it would be okay if she stayed," Irene agreed. "You're right about the fence."

"She'll be fine. Hey, can you imagine what she'll think waking up in a graveyard? Love to see that."

They all laughed.

~~~

Light slowly revealed the cemetery, birds of every calling announcing its arrival. At seven, the gates were unlocked and soon the first visitors began to show up.

Two ladies from Michigan had entered the grounds off Passover Lane and had already taken several snapshots on their phones. One they'd gotten of a tombstone had been especially hilarious and was immediately sent to a friend back home. It read 'I told you I was sick'. They were finding the cemetery to be just as the lady at their guest house had promised—one surprise after another.

They just hadn't expected to find a girl's body stretched out on a crypt, though.

~~~

Homicide Detective Colin Doyle waited for the main gate to be opened and then drove through, passing the U.S.S. Maine Monument to turn left on Second Avenue. Up ahead a KWPD patrol car had parked to the side of the lane. Doyle pulled in behind it and stopped. Several uniformed officers stood in a spot about fifteen feet away. One of them walked over to him.

"I'm Doyle," he said, holding up his ID for the cop to see. "Cemetery secured?"

"Closed up tight, detective. All the gates are locked. Body's over there."

He pointed to where the others stood.

"Get everyone away," Doyle shouted, motioning with his hand. "It's a crime scene, for Christ's sake. Has the ME been called?"

"On the way."

The officer led Doyle to the above ground vault. A female lay on its cement top, placed on her back with her hands across her chest. Slitted eyes half open, an ugly bruise on her left temple.

Doyle bent down for a closer look.

"We need someone to put up an awning to protect the site," he called to the cop. "That sun's brutal."

~~~

Irene Evans had felt better but the shower had helped somewhat. She checked the time. Less than two hours before she's supposed to be at work. Where was Rebecca?

They should never have left her. What were they thinking? Well, that was just it, they weren't thinking. Too much wine, too much weed. Now her friend's missing. Was she still there? She was pretty much out of it. Could be sleeping it off. She looked at her watch again. If she left now, she could go by the cemetery on the way to the Bight.

~~~

"The blow to the head probably killed her," the medical examiner offered. "I'll know exactly after the postmortem, of course. Interesting how she was laid out. Think you've got a sicko here, detective."

Doyle cleared his throat.

"How soon can you autopsy?" he asked.

"Might have you something tomorrow. Okay if we remove the body now?"

"Yeah, I want to check around the area some more. We found a couple of plastic cups. Might've been partying here. According to patrol, there'd been complaints."

~~~

Irene was puzzled by the cemetery being closed. She knocked on the door of the sexton's office and went inside.

"Yes, ma'am," a man said, sitting at a desk. "Can I help you?"

"I was just curious," Irene smiled nervously. "Why isn't the cemetery open?"

"Police closed it today, ma'am. Someone discovered a dead person at one of the graves."

"Is that supposed to be some kind of a joke?" Irene huffed in an annoyed tone. Her anxiety was getting the upper hand.

"No, ma'am, not a joke. A young lady was found lying on top of a crypt. Think she might've been murdered."

Irene's breath left her.

~~~

Charley Wright had lucked out big time. Vacationers had been hitting the silk all day on the parachute boat. He'd made over a hundred bucks in tips. And had gotten the phone number of this really hot chick staying at the Ocean House. Perfect timing, too, because things had been cooling off lately between Rebecca and him.

He wondered how she'd made out last night. Waking up in the cemetery. What a scream, literally. He laughed to himself. Well, maybe she shouldn't drink so much. Speaking of which, how about a drink? Bill should be on duty by now. He walked to the Straw Hat.

"'S'up, Bill?" he asked, settling on a favorite stool.

"Double shifts today," Bill groused. "That big-ass cruise liner docked this morning. Boss called me in. New guy quit."

Bill popped open a beer and slid it to Charley.

"Hear from the girls?" he asked.

"Not a peep. I stopped by their dock to see if they wanted to come. Captain said they didn't show up today. Had to split the crew with the other boat. Pissed off all the hell about it, too. Don't blame him."

"Maybe you should call Irene," Bill said.

~~~

Irene sat in her apartment waiting for her phone to stop ringing. Then she listened to it go to message.

"Hey, Irene. Charley. Just tried to call Rebecca and couldn't get an answer. Now you. What's up, babe? Give me a ring. I'm with Bill."

That was the fifth call today. Four from her boss at work. One from some creep she'd met on a sunset cruise and had stupidly given him her number. She turned off the phone.

She had spent all day trying to find out about the dead girl at the cemetery. Called the police once but hung up before they answered. Suppose it *was* Rebecca. Then what? They'd be all over them asking questions. That cop car hadn't been looking for a donut shop. They were onto someone partying out there.

Maybe Rebecca is mad because they'd left her. Decided to let them worry a while. She wouldn't put it past her. She can be such a little bitch when she wants.

The thing is, she was scared. But staying cooped up in her apartment wasn't going to solve anything. Now she was in big trouble at work, too. She might as well go to the bar.

~~~

"Just thought I'd give you a preliminary update on our victim, detective," the medical examiner said. "Female, appears to be in her early twenties, seemingly good health. No signs of sexual abuse. No defensive wounds on the hands or arms, either. Skull crushed. Blunt instrument would be my guess. Probably never knew what hit her. Blood alcohol index at zero-one-two. Haven't done a drug screen yet."

Doyle nodded. He was in the detective's room at

the KWPD station.

"Thanks a lot, doc. Actually, I have an ID on the lady. We found a billfold at the base of the crypt. Most likely fell out when she was lifted to the top. Name's Rebecca Sloan. Send the prints you've taken from the body to state motor vehicles. I'm sure they'll match the ones on her drivers license."

The ME said he'd have more information tomorrow and wished him good luck. Doyle had already put the prints they'd gotten from the plastic cups into the system but hadn't had a hit yet. He'd had a couple of officers rummage through the trash cans at the cemetery. They'd found a couple of empty wine bottles. Those were being checked for prints, as well. The detective left to check the address he had on Rebecca.

~~~

"Look, we don't know anything so stop worrying," Bill told Irene. "It's probably just like you said. She's way pissed off and is making us pay. Have another drink."

Irene sat at the end of the bar with Charley. The place was crowded and Bill had his hands full trying to keep up. She leaned across the bar.

"I'm telling you that girl they found is Rebecca," she hissed in his ear. "Next, the cops are going to be questioning us."

"Why would they want to do that?" Bill asked. "They don't know we were there."

"Oh, yeah?" Irene said. "That cop car had to know something was going on. We could have been seen leaving."

"Maybe she's right, Bill," Charley agreed. "But even if it is Rebecca, we didn't have anything to do with what happened. She was okay when we left."

Irene glared at him.

"Do you realize we were the last people to see her alive," she said. "Don't you ever watch any cop shows? That's the first thing they say."

"What does that mean," Charley sneered.

"It means we're suspects, Charley."

"No way."

"Yes way," Irene said. "And here's something else to stick in your thick head. Suppose one of us went back? Just saying. But you can bet your ass the cops will be thinking that."

"That's sick, Irene. Do you believe what she just said, Bill?"

Bill went to serve a customer at the other end of the bar.

~~~

Rebecca's address was an apartment building with six units. The mailbox showed her name in number six. Another name with it. Irene Evans. Doyle climbed the steps to the third floor and knocked on the door.

After several more raps, a middle-aged woman opened the door to the apartment across the hall.

"They aren't home," she said.

Doyle held up his ID.

"My name is Detective Colin Doyle. I'm with the Key West police. Rebecca Sloan lives here?"

"Oh, is this about the noise? Guess one of the other neighbors must've complained."

"No, another matter."

"I told them both if they kept it up, somebody was going to call the cops. This is a quiet building."

Doyle smiled.

"Lot of partying?"

"More like a lot of yelling back and forth. Not that I'm nosy but I think it had to do with their job."

"Do you know what kind of work they do?"

"On one of the sunset cruise boats down at the Bight."

"Thank you, ma'am. If you see either one, please have her call me."

He gave her his card.

"I hope you'll say something to them about the noise," she said. "They seem to be nice enough girls."

Doyle knew he wouldn't likely be saying anything to Rebecca Sloan. He drove to the Bight on another chance and got lucky the first try.

Tied to the dock was the two-mast schooner Horizon. Someone was on its deck.

"Good afternoon," Doyle called. "Got a minute?"

He introduced himself to the man and asked if he knew the two women.

"Rebecca and Irene? Yeah, they work for me. I'm the captain of this boat. But right now, both of them are up shit's creek."

"Why is that?"

"Neither one showed up today. Busy as hell, too. Tell you the truth, I'm letting Irene go. Been a little trouble lately."

"Trouble with Irene?"

"Don't have any absolute proof but someone's has been stealing from the tip jar. Word going around is it's

Irene. Rebecca's the better worker anyway."

"I understand they are friends, roommates even," Doyle said. "Might cause some friction."

"Well, in my experience, a job trumps friendship."

Doyle thanked the man and gave him a card and the same request. Call me.

"You never said what this was about," the man smiled.

"Gathering information. Thanks again."

~~~

The *Key West Citizen* had the word out the next morning. Spread across the front page and with photographs of the cemetery. Irene couldn't keep her eyes off of them.

She'd gone home late last night and had gotten in without the nosy neighbor hearing. She had also slipped out quietly this morning. She'd made up what she considered was a great excuse for not showing up at work yesterday and had her fingers crossed that it'd be good enough. But the heartless fuck of a captain hadn't given her a chance to explain before saying she was fired.

So now she was having a coffee at little place on Caroline Street, after first having had a good cry. When she'd picked up the newspaper lying on a table, the tears had come again. Once she had gotten herself together, she'd read the article. No question, it was Rebecca. As if she'd had any doubt. That stupid Charley and Bill denying that anything had happened. Would that've made it go away?

One thing for certain—the police would be at her apartment. She would have to answer their questions sooner or later. Why was she so afraid? She'd had nothing to do with anything. Still, she was frightened out of her wits. What she'd said about them all being suspects? Well, suppose one of them really *had* done it? The tears came again.

She left the coffee shop and walked toward Simonton. Maybe she would just spend the day at Lagerhead's Bar and enjoy the beach.

~~~

Charley Wright hadn't read the newspaper. He'd spent most of the day on the water and now had a roll of bills to show for it. He'd also phoned the hot girl at Ocean House but discovered she'd checked out. No sense in wasting a good night, he'd figured. After showering, he'd slipped on a fresh shirt and shorts and went to the bar.

"You just missed the crowd," Bill said, as Charley pulled up a stool.

"Fine by me, man. I've been running all day."

"See the paper?" Bill asked.

Charley shrugged.

"Better read it," Bill said seriously, laying a copy on the bar. "That was Rebecca at the cemetery."

~~~

A huge buildup of cumulus clouds blanketed the eastern sky and the wind shifted and picked up. Irene wrapped herself in a towel. A few of her beachgoer friends had already left. She was still in a pout about losing her job. It was so unfair.

She knew about the tip jar. She knew who was dipping in it, too. Sweet little Rebecca. She should've gone straight to the captain. Instead, she'd spoken with her about it. How dumb was that? Apparently, Rebecca had put the bad word out on her. Well, what goes around comes around.

Rain pelted. She gathered up her things and ran for shelter.

~~~

"It's going to be a big one," Charley said. "Look at that radar."

Bill had turned the television to the weather station.

"Think the police will want to talk to us?" Charley asked picking up the paper again.

"Fuck, right now I've got bigger issues," Bill said. "The owner's pulling an audit."

"So what?"

"So all those bottles of wine we drank at the cemetery are going to be on me," Bill said. "That's what for a start."

"Can't be that much."

"You'd be surprised."

"I'm going to split, man," Charley said. "Try to beat the storm home before it gets worse."

The other customers cleared out after Charley had gone. Bill wiped down the bar and restocked the beer cooler. He noticed some water pooling from beneath a cabinet. The damn roof leaking again. He'd talked with the owner more than once about getting it repaired. All he could do at the present was stay clear of it. The rain was really coming down now. It was dark as night outside.

The door opened and a man came in. He was wearing a black plastic garbage bag over his clothes with holes punched out for his head and arms. His baseball cap was soaked. He was barefoot.

Bill looked up, surprised.

"Hello, Bill."

"What do you want? You know you're not welcome here."

"I've come to finish the game," Walt Devany said with a grin. "Just you and me now."

"You better leave," Bill said, grabbing up his phone, "or I'll call the cops."

Walt slipped a .38 snub nose revolver from his pocket, cocked the hammer and pointed it at Bill, all in one quick move.

"Ease off the phone, son," he said.

Bill placed it on the bar.

"You're crazy," he muttered.

"Got that right," Walt laughed. "Crazy was my charm. When we were friends, remember? Always got a big laugh out of Walt and I was happy to oblige. Then I found out what kind of friends you bunch really was. Thought your crap didn't stink. You were always laughing, yeah, but it was *at* me and my funny ways, not *with* me."

"Nobody really meant anything, Walt."

"Sometimes all it takes is a little."

"C'mon, man. Put that thing down and let me buy you a drink."

Bill was beginning to sweat.

"Even took the hit for your drug dealing, Bill. Cost me about all I had—my job, my room, my other so-called friends. But everything stayed cozy with you. Drinking and drugging at the cemetery. Playing the game."

"Not my fault you got busted, Walt," Bill said nervously.

"Sure it is, Bill. You, Charley, Irene, Rebecca. You all gave me up."

"Walt, this is stupid," Bill said. "I'm sorry about what happened but that's over."

"Over is right," Walt laughed.

Bill looked at him, puzzled.

"I've been watching, Bill. Standing in the shadow of love, like the song goes. I knew you'd be at the cemetery. New moon. I was there, too. Close enough to smell the weed, to hear your high-pitched shitty laughter, to reach out and touch you. Almost next to you but you were too stoned to notice."

"Be careful with that gun, Walt. Let's talk."

Walt laughed again.

"You played the game. Rebecca said she was going in her sleep. Charley drowned. Irene stabbed in the heart. Me, electrocuted. And you, good buddy? Shot."

He raised the gun, his finger on the trigger.

"Pow!" he said aloud.

Bill turned his head, wincing.

"Couldn't believe you left Rebecca there," he continued. "Made it so easy for me. Irene and Charley not much of a problem, either. Move back toward the cash register, Bill."

"Don't do this, Walt," Bill cried.

"Just like you said, Bill, you died a hero trying to stop a robber."

Walt stepped around the bar and put his foot in a puddle of water. A huge jolt of electricity from the frayed wire inside the cabinet instantly shot up his leg. He was already dead when the gun went off.

~~~

The first responders called detectives. Two dead bodies. One shot, the other unknown. Later that same night, a woman's body was found behind a shed at Simonton beach. She'd been stabbed. And the next day, a man's body was fished out of the Bight. Apparently he'd struck his head and drowned.

It was one for the books.

As the Night
Went On

Harry Schroeder

As the night went on, the talk turned to death, and
the mood changed, full of a mordant energy, the
stories bouncing back and forth between horror and a
high black humor, the sort of thing men do who've seen
a lot of death, not to deny it, just to hold it off, bring it
down at least for a moment to where they can feel on
top of it. Paul told about the rock star who had it in his
will to be cremated and his ashes mixed in with a pound
of the best Jamaican, so his friends could smoke him.
Duane, who was from Texas, mentioned the retarded
man on Death Row he had heard about down home,
who got it into his head that he was being executed
because he was illiterate, and spent all his time in his
cell desperately trying to teach himself to read so they
wouldn't kill him. Jackson spoke of a street dealer he
knew who ripped off his suppliers. "They took him out
to sea, chained him into a cork ring life preserver, sliced
his thighs and his ball sack to put blood in the water,
and tossed him overboard," he said. "The top half of
him drifted in to shore later on, dried out and burnt
black, bobbing around in the life preserver like some
kid's bathtub toy. Nobody ever figured out which got
him first, the sun or the sharks." "A life preserver," Paul

said, thoughtfully. "Well, O.K. ... I guess." I considered mentioning some of martyred saints – Hippolytus torn apart by horses, Lawrence on the grille, Sebastian used for target practice by Diocletian's archers – but decided that they were doing well enough without me. Willie told the story of a huge jet he'd seen in the private section of an airport, the plane serving as a traveling palace for the ruler of one of the Arab oil countries. "It had a throne room, with a throne on a gimbal," he told us, "so that it was always facing Mecca. And it had a medical and surgical facility on it, with a staff checked out to do any kind of operation, even a heart transplant." He paused, for effect, grinning. "And the emir traveled with his own heart donor." That stopped everyone for a moment, and then there was a set of angry protests. "Christ," Jackson burst out. "He kept another guy around for spare parts?" Paul ended it with the story of Old Joe, the town drunk in the little Ohio town where he grew up, who was found dead in a doorway one late fall morning. The town had no public funds for burials, so they turned the corpse over to Perkins, the local undertaker, to deal with it. "A week later Joe showed up in the funeral parlor's picture window," Paul said, "as an advertisement for the high quality work Perkins did, dressed in white tie and tails, sitting in a rocking chair with his legs crossed at the knee, holding a plastic lily. Stuffed." "Stuffed?" Jackson asked indignantly. "Stuffed? You mean, like – taxidermy?" "Stuffed," Paul said. "The city fathers went crazy, but Perkins hung in there – they'd given him the body, he said, and it was his property to do what he wanted with. So Joe stayed right there in the picture window, for years. Kids would steal him in his chair and set him rocking on people's porches and ring the doorbell, and once, at Halloween, they stuck him in the middle of the main street in town with bat wings on his shoulders and a fright wig on his head and a pumpkin in his lap.

"He stayed there in that picture window, for years, getting a little more frayed and moth-eaten every year. Finally Perkins retired and sold his shop, and the new undertaker had no place for the likes of Old Joe. So he threw him out, along with all the other junk he found." Jackson was furious. "Threw him out? Just like that?" "Right," Paul said. "Stuck him on top of a G.I. can out back, for the garbage truck. And the garbagemen came and just tossed him up onto the truck, and it was at the end of their route, and they went through town to the dump with Old Joe sitting there in plain sight on top of all the garbage, with people staring and kids yelling and dogs barking alongside. He ended up as part of a landfill. Later on I heard they built a suburban housing development on it." No one said anything, thinking about that. Then, almost in unison, they got up to leave.

About The Authors

1
R.K. Simpson

R.K. Simpson lives in Alexandria, Virginia, with his wife Patty. He is a graduate of Dartmouth College and a veteran of the Marine Corps and the war in Vietnam. He served as a diplomat in several of our embassies in Europe and Africa for over twenty years. Upon retiring from the government, he worked as a pediatric nurse for fifteen years. He has three adult children.

2
Brewster Chamberlin

    Unable to break into the tenured groves of academe, despite a solid and well-received doctoral dissertation, Brewster Chamberlin spent several decades of his life working as a historian, archivist, university teacher, lecturer, poet, essayist and writer of longer and shorter fictions while living in Manhattan, Germany, France (Provence), Italy, Washington DC and Greece. In 2001 he retired from an executive position at the U.S. Holocaust Memorial Museum in Washington DC to move with his wife Lynn-Marie Smith to Key West, Florida, to concentrate on a series of novels.

3.
Shirrel Rhoades

    Shirrel Rhoades is a writer, critic, filmmaker, former college professor, art collector, museum president, and publisher. These days, he calls Key West home. He is the author of *Four Fingers Four Minute Mysteries, The Devil's Hop Yard,* and *Front Row at the Movies*, among other titles. He and his wife share their historic classic temple revival style house in Old Town with a dog and ½ cat and sometimes even a pretty TV morning show host. But that's another story.

4.
Andrew Daly

Andrew Daly is originally from Port Orchard, Washington. A 20-year veteran of the U.S.C.G. He served on ships, life boat stations and shore assignments in Alaska, the Oregon Coast, Europe and North Atlantic, the Caribbean, the Mississippi River, the Texas desert and Key West prior to retirement in 1995. He then became a civilian federal employee travelling extensively in the Caribbean and Central America until retirement in 2015. He holds a B.A. from the Evergreen State College and an M.PA from the University of Maryland (Baltimore). He is married to the former Carolyn Dewey. He is currently pursuing the art of uselessness and intends to master it, eventually.

5.
Bill Craig

Bill Craig taught himself to read at age four and began writing his own stories at age six. He published his first novel at age 40 and says it only took him 34 years to become an overnight success! He has been publishing steadily ever since that first book *Valley of Death*. The latest entry in his bestselling Key West mystery series is *Marlow: Papa's Legacy*.

6.
Justin Maxwell

Justin Maxwell is the pen name of Wayne "Skip" Kadar. He taught at the high school level for several years then became a high school principal. After 16 years as a principal he retired from education. In retirement he worked as a harbor master at a marina on the Great Lakes and researched and wrote eight historically factual books about the Great Lakes region; books about ships that now lie on the bottom of the freshwater seas.

7·
Barthélemy Banks

Barthélemy Banks is the *nom de plume* of a former supervisor for a publishing company that was secretly backed by the CIA. He spent a number of years in the Bahamas where he rubbed elbows with spies, smugglers, international bankers, and reclusive millionaires. Today, he lives on a remote island, where he finds it safe to write about the clandestine world he knows so well.

8.
Jack Mazur

Jack Mazur studied creative writing at Southern Connecticut State University in the 1980s under Richard Russo, who would go on to win the Pulitzer for *Empire Falls* in 2005 or so.

9.
Robert Coburn

Robert Coburn is originally from Norfolk, Virginia. After high school in Norfolk, he spent three years in the US Army as a helicopter crew chief stationed in Berlin, Germany. He returned home to attend college at Richmond Professional Institute (Now VCU) in Richmond, Virginia, where he earned a Bachelor of Science degree in Advertising. He also met his wife in Richmond while a student there.

Coburn has worked at major advertising agencies in New York and Los Angeles. His ads have won top awards both nationally and internationally. He is an instrument rated commercial pilot and plays saxophone. He and his wife now live in Carmel, California.

10.
Harry Schroeder

After getting advanced degrees from Yale and Harvard, Harry Schroeder taught college English for ten years. He dropped out of academia to Key West in 1979, where he made his living driving a cab for twelve years, doing some drug counseling at a lockdown program for teenagers, delivering papers, writing music criticism for local weeklies, and in music, as a trombonist and arranger. Eventually he went back to college teaching, at St. Leo's on the Navy base here. Now he teaches, works on a novel, and makes music: he may have the distinction of being the oldest musician ever to go on the road with a rock band.

ABSOLUTELY AMA⚡ING eBOOKS